"Y... the book of my life and jump right into the middle of it,"

Trey Blackfox said as he leaned in a little farther into her personal space.

"Don't worry, *The Autobiography of a Serial Dater* isn't on my reading list," Sasha quipped.

Trey chuckled and the sound magically dissipated the knot that had formed in her stomach from the moment he'd crowded into the car.

"Actually, *The Trials and Tribulations of Being the Youngest Son* is the story of my life."

"You don't look traumatized to me," Sasha said.

"It's the years of therapy," he replied.

"And which kind did you have—shock or psychoanalysis?"

While he searched for a snappy comeback, Trey's legs spread out and their knees touched for a moment. Sasha almost spilled her drink. The brief contact sent a shiver through her body. It had been too long a time since a man's touch had triggered a reaction in her....

ANGELA WEAVER

is a Southern girl by way of Tennessee. She's lived in Philadelphia, Atlanta, Washington, D.C., New York and Tokyo, Japan. An avid reader and occasional romantic optimist, she began writing her first novel on a dare and hasn't stopped since. Having heeded the call to come home to the South, she has returned to Atlanta. On weekends, she can be found hiking in the North Georgia Mountains, scuba diving or working on her next book.

Angela Weaver

A LOVE
TO REMEMBER

KIMANI
ROMANCE

My idea of friendship is
Not the easiest to understand
Or to embrace
Some have come
And others have gone
This book is for Mrs. B, Courtney B and Latoya K
When I wish for laughter, love, advice, inspiration
or to share some pain
You are my blessing

Thank you.

 KIMANI PRESS™

ISBN-13: 978-1-58314-791-7
ISBN-10:   1-58314-791-8

A LOVE TO REMEMBER

www.kimanipress.com

Printed in U.S.A.

Dear Reader,

I hope that when you close the book with the end of Trey and Sasha's story, you'll do so with a smile on your face and twinkle in your eye. And although their youngest brother has settled into blissful domesticity, Caleb Blackfox and Marius Blackfox are still in for romantic challenges in their lives. I hope you'll join me in my next book featuring Caleb and Miranda Tyler's story.

Miranda Tyler had tried her best never to set foot back in her hometown of Cartersville, Georgia. But after her older brother's injury in a car accident, the analyst for the U.S. Department of Justice is back...but, she's not alone. Charged with the responsibility of hiding a ten-year-old witness in a high-profile murder case, Miranda is dead set on avoiding the one man she's never forgot. But when Caleb Blackfox learns that his first love is back in town, he's determined to pull out all the stops to keep Miranda safe and in his arms for a lifetime.

I enjoy writing about love and sharing my stories with you. I also enjoy hearing from you, so please feel free to e-mail me (angela@angelaweaver.com) or to check out my Web site at www.angelaweaver.com.

Smiles,

Angela Weaver

Acknowledgments

Some of you say, "Joy is greater than sorrow,"
and others say, "Nay, sorrow is the greater."
But I say unto you, they are inseparable.
Together they come, and when one sits alone
with you at your board, remember that the other
is asleep upon your bed.

—The Prophet

Chapter 1

Malay Peninsula, Southeast Asia

"Tell me this isn't a mirage and that I won't wake up with snakes or lizards in my sleeping bag," Thorne demanded for the second time.

"This isn't a mirage. We're actually here," Sasha replied to the wildlife photographer. A second later, her hands finally found the right combination to unfold the portable canvas chair. Even under the shade of the high trees and a tent top, the humidity of the rainforest had beads of sweat popping up all over her forehead. For the third time that afternoon, she longingly thought of her last trip to the Australian Outback. Having flown from an oven to a sauna, she preferred the former to the latter. No matter how much she tried to keep cool and dry, nothing worked. Any day now, she expected fungus to start growing on her khakis and cotton shirt.

"Okay…okay," he rushed. "Now tell me again that we're getting paid for this trip."

"We will be paid once we complete the assignment," she carefully explained. Graced with movie-star looks, blue eyes, curly flaxen hair and an ability to be at the right place at the right time with the right photographic equipment, Thorne Roswell could have pursued a career in fashion or commercial photography. Yet, like her, his love of animals and conservation drove him to seek out some of the world's most elusive wildlife.

"*All* expenses?" he pressed.

Sasha turned around and backed into the less than sturdy chair. It was their eighth day of a month-long expedition and they had a few hours before the subject of her study appeared to take a drink from the nearby river. Until then they would wait. "Every cent."

"In U.S. dollars?"

"Nope." She allowed a satisfied glance to grace her lips. The foundation funding their trip was located in the United Kingdom. After a few days of wrangling, she'd been lucky enough to get them to agree to settle the contract in the local currency. "British pounds."

Several moments passed and she could imagine the photographer's mind calculating the currency conversion as he pulled out a camera lens from his backpack.

"Tell me again that this isn't a mirage."

She chuckled and reached up to push a stray braid behind her ear. "The money will be in your bank account before the plane comes back to pick us up."

"And I don't have to go to some bottom-tier university and lecture to class after class of pill-popping, Internet-addicted, know-it-all undergraduate students?"

"Not this time," Sasha answered. "We just have to combine your photographs with my research, present our finding to the group and turn in our material."

Thorne placed his hands behind this head and leaned back. The camera lens lay forgotten in his lap. "Sasha, my girl, this is the life. Perfect weather, fresh air, civilization is miles away and we're getting paid to lie in the shade."

Perfect. The word echoed in her head. As far as she was concerned the Malay Peninsula was far from the garden of Eden. The Bible had mentioned only one snake in Genesis. So far, she'd encountered over a dozen. "Don't forget we've got a job to do."

"Yeah, and as long as the tapir hides in the bushes, we wait."

"I hate waiting," she stated.

"I really don't mind it at all." He grinned.

Sasha looked upward to the center section of the tent and held in a sigh. "Somehow that doesn't surprise me," she replied.

Thorne shrugged his shoulders. "Out of the practically overflowing list of bug-infested, end-of-the-world locales you've chosen for us to research, this is a virtual paradise."

Paradise. She shook her head at the word. They had arrived in the southern edge of Malaysia only two weeks ago. The land was as untamed and wild as she'd imagined and just as beautiful. Sunrise that morning had been spectacular, brilliant oranges and blues lighting up the clouds. The verdant trees and low hanging patches of fog made it look like a painting without frames. Although the scenery appealed to her on every level, the small details like oppressive heat and the smell of rotting vegetation was never far from her thoughts.

Sasha resisted the urged to pull up her pants leg and scratch the tiny red bumps left by a matching pair of leech bites. Every couple of hours, they would have to check the tents for the most miniscule of holes. In this jungle, one small hole served as a neon open sign to the entire insect population in the area. And she'd had enough of biting ants to last an eternity.

The last instance she'd been less conscientious, she'd woken up in the middle of the night to see a flood of hundreds of ants sweeping over the equipment like a wave of brown water. Outnumbered, she'd had to abandon her tent and slept in the Jeep.

"Glad you like the neighborhood," she replied. "Why don't you stay?" The sarcastic undertone in her voice was completely lost on Thorne. It had taken her a few months, but she'd gotten used to the wildlife photographer's constant need to compliment or complain.

"I'm serious," he continued. "This is the best place you've dragged me to yet."

"I did not drag you anywhere. You practically begged me to get you on the first plane flying so you could hide from your mother and the vindictive girl-friend who caught you in bed with another woman."

Sasha opened her eyes and peered out the opaque camouflage color of the mosquito netting. Less than a hundred yards away, elephants had joined hippos in the slow running river.

"Wrong, I only took this job because no one in their right mind would spend three weeks with you. You, Sasha, rarely talk, don't drink, don't smoke and don't go out to clubs. Honestly, love, you have the social skills of a Tasmanian Devil."

Sasha didn't say a word. What could she say? Thorne was right. She didn't like being around a lot of people and talking was a waste of energy. She'd seen the effects of alcohol too many times to want to partake.

The familiar high-pitched sound of a female mosquito prompted her to roll down her sleeves and turn toward Thorne as he lay sprawled out on the tent's tarmac. She gestured toward one of the bags. "Hey, can you pass the repellant? We've got a hungry guest."

"You didn't forget to take your malaria pill this morning, did you?" he asked.

"Thorne." She said his name slowly as he continued to dig through the bag. "I reminded you to take the pill."

"Right."

Sasha shook the bottle of concentrated bug spray and proceeded to squirt it on the exposed sections of her skin, then she put her research notebook to the side, and completely relaxed in the chair. The little voice in the back of her mind whispered that she should have been entering in more information, but instead she lay back.

With her eyes closed against the warmth of the afternoon sun, Sasha inhaled deeply and smiled at her colleague's relaxed comment.

Their sole purpose was to study the very elusive and near-extinct Malayan tapirs. The nocturnal and reclusive donkey-size animal inhabited only select parts of the tropical forest. They'd been in the target habitat a week and had only seen footprints of the beast. If she hadn't seen a black and white photo taken a few months before by another expedition, she would have given up and moved on to the next project. However seductive the lush tropical weather and abundant the wildlife population, the overabundance of insects still made her want to head to cooler climates. Overhead the trill sound of a bird echoed and a breeze carrying the scent of decaying vegetation made Sasha wrinkle her nose.

At thirty-one, most of her college classmates had settled into comfortable corporate or public careers, married and begun saving for a future child's education.

Sasha, on the other hand, wasn't looking. An ironic smile appeared and quickly disappeared; she'd had marriage offers from men on three continents. The first time, she hadn't even hit puberty. During an expedition in Kenya, her parents' guide had offered her father over a hundred cows. She leaned back and again closed her eyes. Several minutes passed and she'd begun to drift into a light doze when Thorne called her name.

"Sasha."

"What?" She opened her eyes slightly.

"Did you hear that?"

"Thorne, how many times do I have to tell you that the local snakes aren't poisonous and they won't come near you, much less bite?"

"Exactly twenty-three. But that's not it."

His powers of observation worked great when they were tracking a subject, but at times like this he made her want to scream. "Then what is it?"

"Listen."

Sasha stood up and focused her attention outward. Straining her ears, she concentrated on putting aside the white noise of the forest. And the same moment, she picked up the whirring noise; every animal alongside the stream seemed to freeze. Sasha's heart stuttered to a stop and then jerked into high speed.

"Damn," she swore. "That sounds like…"

"A plane," he stated simply.

"What would it be doing way out here?"

He shrugged and stood up. "Maybe poachers?"

"Not likely," she growled. "They'd come over land. From the sound of it, I think the plane is headed toward us."

Sasha's gaze narrowed on the milling animals. This deep into the tropical forest, most of the animals had not been exposed to humans or machines. It suddenly occurred to her that the sound of the plane would inevitably trigger the "fight or flight" instinct inherent in most living things. "We need to gather everything we can and get behind the trees."

"They may run the other way." Thorne came to stand alongside her.

"Do you want to put your life and our equipment at risk?"

"So now you're the rhinoceros expert, too?" Thorne said sarcastically. The twang of his cockney accent came out in full force. "You think they're going to stampede."

"I know they will." Sasha drew in a deep breath and let it out slowly.

She moved quickly to pick up the equipment and dump it in the travel bags. The entire episode reminded her of why she preferred the company of animals to humans. She'd had her pick of group expeditions, but it hadn't taken her long to realize she'd inherited her parents' solitary nature.

Sasha didn't look at Thorne. If she didn't need his talent, she would have stopped using his services long ago. She'd learned from her parents how to take care of herself in any environment. But what she hadn't learned, and it would irritate her for life, was how to deal with people. And that undeniable fact made it easy for her to work and live in undeveloped countries and remote locales around the world on a moment's notice.

"Move it," she ordered, stuffing the GPS system, radio, laptop and video set into another bag. "Or someone's going to find your trampled corpse."

She grabbed her backpack and pushed through the tent flap. Her eyes scanned the horizon even as her ears could more easily detect the whirring sound. Sasha took off in the direction of more heavily wooded area with Thorne right behind her. Only when they'd gotten deep enough into the overgrown thicket of trees and underbrush did she slow down. A few minutes later when she was sure that they would safe, she stopped and dropped her bags onto the floor.

"We'll wait here for at least a half hour."

Breathing heavily, Thorne just nodded his head and slowly collapsed under the weight of his equipment bags. Turning her face towards the sky, her eyes strained to catch a glimpse of the horizon through the thick foliage. Failing to see anything, she used her ears and hands instead. Sasha crouched and out her hand against the ground. Sure enough, she could feel the slight trembling that had nothing to do with earthquakes and more to do with large stampeding herds.

Not this way, she prayed silently. The Lord must have been listening as the plane approached along with the animals because, as she'd hoped, the thick brush and trees forced them to go around their location.

"Good thinking," Thorne whispered.

Sasha noticed the beads of sweat rolling off his forehead, and didn't say a word.

An hour later after having returned to their campsite and discovered it intact, Sasha leaned down next to the abandoned lagoon and lifted a black plastic cylinder from the rocky shore. She held the object far from her body and stared at it. Her name had been stenciled in bold white letters on the side. Whatever it contained was important enough to have someone hire a plane to deliver it. A shiver raced down her spine with a shadow of foreboding. Drawing in a calm breath, she unscrewed the top and pulled out three sheets of heavy paper.

Several heartbeats passed as she read through the missive, and uncaring of the muddy water seeping between her toes, she dropped the container. Clutching the papers to her chest, Sasha walked back toward the undisturbed campsite and stopped as her knees threatened to buckle. She caught sight of Thorne just as he finished taking a drink of water from one of the many canteens. "We need to pack up," she said in a low voice.

"What?"

She avoided eye contact by looking over his shoulder. "We're leaving,"

"What did you just say?" he questioned. "I swear you just said that we were leaving."

"I did."

"Just like that? A little stampede has scared the unflappable Sasha Clayton?"

"I have to go back to the States."

"What the hell is so bloody important that someone sent a plane into the middle of a tropical forest?"

"That's my business." Careful not to look Thorne in the face, her eyes went from his ear to his neck. Grief welled in the center of her throat and tears threatened to overflow from her eyes at any moment. And just looking at him might set her off.

"It's my livelihood and reputation. If you're going to bail out the least you can do is tell me why."

Sasha lowered her eyes to the ground as dozens of should haves and could haves crowded into her head all at once.

"He's dead."

"Good God," Thorne rushed. "Your father's passed away?"

Instinctually, she pushed the thought of her father's mortality away. "No, my godfather."

"I'm sorry, love."

From the corners of her eyes, Sasha glimpsed the photographer shift back and forth with indecision. He didn't know whether to comfort her with a hug or take another step back. Although they came from separate continents and had radically different experiences growing up, it hadn't taken Sasha long to notice the big similarity: neither of them dealt well with the human species in emotional situations.

In a somber voice, he said, "Sasha, there's no way you can make it back to the States for the funeral."

The uncharacteristically strained tone in his voice derailed her train of thought. She simply nodded her head. "I know."

Sasha's knees could no longer bear the weight of her sorrow. Her knees gave out and she collapsed back against a tree. Ignoring Thorne completely, she lost herself with precious memories of Uncle Camden. Eight months ago, he had surprised her by showing up in England on the very day of her acceptance into the Zoological Academy. Just last month, she'd called to wish him happy birthday. She'd begun to end the conversation with "I love you." But he hadn't heard it because the line had been disconnected.

Only with the sudden loss did she come to grips with the depth of emotions for her sixty-year-old godfather. Grief consumed her. She wanted to share more time with him. She wanted Uncle Camden to be her guide again like he was years ago, as they explored the rainforests and Mayan ruins of Belize; when they ran from alligators, camped on barges and tracked black howler monkeys for two weeks. She wanted to eat peanut butter sandwiches and drink coffee so strong that it doubled as an insect repellant. Her sorrow deepened and memories gave way to tears.

"I'll start packing," Thorne volunteered.

"Thank you," she whispered. The finality of the moment weighed on her shoulders. She thought about her parents, her great aunt Margaret and her best friend, Lena. The images of all her loved ones flashed through her mind. Sasha was no stranger to death. After having spent all of her life observing nature's cycle of birth and death, she'd come to accept it. This time, however, death cut to the bone.

Moments later after she'd managed some semblance of control over her runaway emotions, Sasha stood up and without a word, pushed back the tent flap and stepped inside. "We'll be back soon, Thorne," she said huskily.

However, even as she voiced those words she had a feeling in the bottom of her stomach that it wouldn't be as soon as she hoped.

Chapter 2

Atlanta, Georgia

Two days after learning of her godfather's death, Sasha woke one limb at a time.

The feeling of blood pumping through her veins and the dull ache in her back brought the welcome sensation of being alive. Yet, the source of the pain took her a moment to figure out. Slowly as the haze of sleep began to lift, she realized that for the first time in weeks she'd slept in a bed. Actually, a feather bed with four down pillows, soft cotton sheets and a down comforter.

She opened her eyes and squinted into the darkness before rolling over and reaching. Her long fingers encountered nothing but the soft duvet cover. Sasha looked at the glow of the bedside clock—10:30 a.m. She'd slept three hours, but she felt as if she'd been sleeping for a few minutes. She rolled over again and fumbled around until she managed to locate the switch for the bedside lamp. Low light suffused the room. Thick drapes covered two windows, a flat screen television flanked by heavy dark furniture and crème-colored walls.

Sasha pushed a pillow behind her back and inhaled the lavender scent exuding from the bed sheets. The king-size sleigh bed shouted luxury.

Uneasy, Sasha picked up the telephone and began to dial. Because of the sanctions against Cuba, she had to dial a service in Canada to be rerouted to her parents' new home. A moment of silence passed as the international connection took place. When if finally came, the stuttered ring made her heart slip a beat.

"Hello?" a familiar voice answered.

"Momma."

"Sasha, baby. Where are you?"

She closed her eyes and gripped the phone tighter as her chest tightened. The sound of her mother's voice simultaneously relieved her and reminded Sasha of how much she missed her family. She took a deep breath and steadied her voice before replying. "I'm calling from Atlanta."

"Oh, baby. I've been praying for you since I found out about Camden. How are you?"

She sat up straighter. "I'm okay. Momma, does Dad know about Uncle Camden?"

"We got a letter in the mail about two weeks ago."

Sasha cradled the phone tighter. "Did he come to the funeral?"

"No. I wanted to go, but he wouldn't hear of it."

Part of her wanted to voice the unspoken question of why. Yet, she held back. Her father was a man who lived by simple rules and staunch pride. No matter the history and connection between him and her godfather, Camden Ridgestone's death wouldn't have broken his vow never to see or speak to his best friend again.

"Is he around?"

"He's out checking the caves. Now, how did you find out about Camden's death? I thought you were on an island in the Asia."

"Uncle Camden's attorney tracked me down."

"Why? It would have been impossible for you make it back in time for the funeral."

"I'm required to be at the reading of the will," Sasha responded slowly.

Several heartbeats passed before her mother said, "I don't like the sound of that."

"I'm not sure I like it, either, but I really didn't have a choice. Uncle Camden's attorneys took care of everything from the plane tickets to this hotel suite."

"Hotel suite?"

Sasha smiled and curled her legs under her like a child. "At the Ritz Carlton. The place has a bathroom bigger than my studio in Brooklyn. Not to mention the monogrammed slippers, bathrobes and a Jacuzzi tub."

"Samuel won't like the sound of that."

Sasha automatically tensed at the mention of her father's disapproval. "Mom, I know you don't like to keep secrets, but if you tell Dad that Uncle Camden included me in his will Dad's blood pressure will shoot through the stratosphere."

"I'll let him know you called and that you're all right. But you have to call me back and let me know what's going on."

"Promise. I love you, Momma."

"I love you more, hummingbird."

Sasha's chest suffused with love at the sound of her pet name. She waited for the click on the other end of the line before placing the phone back on its cradle. Sasha slid off the bed and stretched as her toes sunk into the carpet before slipping into the hotel slippers and donning the plush terry bathrobe.

Spying a small counter with a coffee pot, tea and snacks, her stomach growled, reminding Sasha that she hadn't eaten since arriving on the East Coast. Just as she crossed the living area, she heard a knock on the door.

Sasha secured the belt around her robe and opened the door. A hotel attendant smiled and Sasha stepped aside as the man wheeled in a dish-laden cart. "Good morning," she greeted him.

"Morning, I hope you don't mind that I'm a little

late. We had a little problem with the service elevator this morning. But don't let that bother you because the toast should still be warm and the coffee could still scald the living daylights out of a man."

Sasha laughed and shook her head as she let go of the doorknob and let the door swing closed. "I wasn't expecting breakfast, so cold or hot really doesn't matter to me since I'm starving."

Her eyes, which had just minutes before been narrow slits, opened when the smell of fresh roasted coffee wafted into her nostrils. He sat the cart alongside the windows and pushed back the curtains, letting bright sunlight into the room. She crossed the room and picked up one of the silver covers to discover fresh croissants, muffins, toast, fruit and an assortment of jams.

"This is enough to feed a small family."

"The Ritz might be cheap when it comes close to Christmas bonus time, but they don't play around with making the guests feel welcome."

"Would you like to join me for breakfast?"

"You're not from around here, are you?"

"Originally? No. I was born in North Carolina, but I've spent most of my life traveling."

He chuckled and a smile slid up his face. "You know, we're not really supposed to talk to the guests."

Happy to hear American English and be in the company of a fellow person of color, she winked. "I won't tell if you won't. How about a cup of coffee?"

"All right. My name is Frank."

After a half hour of food and conversation, Sasha locked the hotel door behind Frank and made her way to the bathroom. All it took was one quick look into the wall-length mirror to ruin her easy morning. The Senegalese woman who'd braided her hair had done an excellent job. But hiking through tropical forests and moving through thick underbrush had turned her stunning hairstyle into a complete disaster. The cornrows were in dire need of rebraiding. Since that wasn't an option and she didn't possess a proper hat or scarf, she sighed heavily. Sasha sat on top of the closed toilet seat, reached over her head and pursued her only option. Wincing at the thought, she began the two-hour process of unbraiding her hair.

People should be required to give three months' notice before dying.

Sasha reached into her purse, pulled out a small packet of facial tissues, and wiped away a stray tear. So what if dying was an inevitable part of life—her uncle Camden should have told her he was terminally ill with cancer and he was putting her in the will.

Sasha balled the damp tissue in her hand and looked out the window at the passing scenery. The afternoon sunshine felt warm against her skin, but she turned away and closed her eyes. She let the motion of the moving car and butter-soft leather seats against her spine lull her into a calm state. But not even soothing jazz pouring from the invisible back speakers could rid her of the sense of loss and sadness.

She was feeling guilty and angry, and she hated it. Hated that she'd been off on the other side of the world while her godfather had suffered. Hated the fact that she hadn't called or written in over a month. If only she'd known...

Her nails dug into the armrest and she resisted the urge to rub her eyes as she contemplated the remainder of the day. Uncle Camden's attorneys had arranged for the three-hundred-dollar-a-night suite with all the perks money could buy, but she'd barely slept a wink. The idea of spending an afternoon of sitting with people she didn't know and finding out that she might have inherited things that she didn't want had kept her awake throughout the transcontinental flight. Sasha shivered with the thought.

This was the first time in her memory that someone she loved had died. Both her maternal and paternal grandparents had died when she was a baby. Her mother and father had been only children and keeping with what she called the Clayton tradition, Sasha was on only child. Not for lack of trying for a little brother or sister. Her mother's second miscarriage had guaranteed that she would be the only offspring. If the day came that she actually took part in the mating cycle and got married, she vowed to have at least three kids. Every child should have a sibling. Instead of having an older brother or younger sister, she'd been alone. Of course, that meant extra attention from her parents and the undivided love of Uncle Camden, but she could have traded it all to not feel the loneliness she felt at that moment.

"Here we are, miss."

The car stopped and the driver began to unbuckle his seat belt in preparation for opening the door, but Sasha waved him off. "I can get the door."

"Of course, I shall be returning you to the hotel. Please wait in the lobby for me."

"Thank you." Sasha looked the driver again. Short black curly hair with a smattering of silver. She'd been too distracted and upset to pay attention to the man when he'd picked her up at the airport the day before. But now she noticed his British accent. It wasn't the fashionable accent of the international reporters she often met in her travels, but the familiar lilt of Uncle Camden's British lilt. Feeling another bout of weeping coming on, she scrambled out of the car.

Sasha stepped out of the taxi into a landscaped lower plaza. A cold breeze hit her cheek as the car door closed behind her. She pulled the winter air deep into her lungs, let it out slowly and released a smidgen of tension. A clear blue sky complete with tiny dots of clouds reflected off the doors. She instinctively tilted her back and she looked upward over the glass-and-steel structure. Her eyes landed on the top of the building and she blinked in pleasant surprise. Unlike most of the skyscrapers she encountered in her travels,

she didn't find the pointed top. Instead, the building
hosted two half circles like delicate wings curving
toward one another.

Shaking off her thoughts, Sasha gripped her purse
and joined in the stream of people entering the building.
Men and women were dressed in the latest business
wear chic. By the time Sasha made it from the automatic glass doors to the richly appointed elevator lobby,
she'd lost count of the number of designer handbags,
ties, timepieces, cell phones and wireless headsets.

Sasha felt more out of place than ever, not that she
didn't blend in. She'd had her herringbone black suit
custom-made from one of the best tailors in Bangkok.
So what if the Brooks Brothers design was two years
old. Her ex-high school roommate and Manhattan-
dwelling best friend had assured her that a well-made
black suit matched with a cream-colored silk camisole
never went out of style. She followed a group of brief-
case-toting men into the elevator and pressed the button
for one of the higher floors. Briefly glancing at the
LCD panel, she checked the time and the temperature.
A groan welled up in the back of her throat—she was
early. She would have to wait an extra twenty minutes.
She caught an interested glance from one of the male
passengers, and quickly returned her gaze to the door,
before curiosity drew her eyes back. Sure enough, he
was looking right at her. Sasha dropped her gaze again
and barely kept from squirming. He looked to be in his
late thirties with straight brown hair and a curious

twinkle in his green eyes. Like the rest of the group, he wore a blue dress shirt underneath his dark suit jacket.

The number couldn't go up fast enough for Sasha. The sooner she got off the elevator, the sooner she'd find out why her godfather had summoned her to Atlanta, and the sooner she could get back to her work. Correction: the sooner she could get the heck away from all those people. She exhaled, remembering the words from one of her previous therapists. No, she wasn't anti-social; she just hadn't been properly socialized. The elevator stopped and Mr. Green Eyes stepped off. Sasha let out a breath and then pulled it back in as the elevator stopped on her floor. She stepped off onto a plush Persian rug and inhaled. The slightly heavy scent of vanilla made her sneeze.

"Ms. Clayton?"

"Yes?" Sasha looked up from digging into her purse to grab another Kleenex. She wiped her nose and looked in the direction of the female voice that had called her name.

"Good Afternoon. My name is Gretchen Stevens. I'm Mr. Hawthorne's executive assistant."

She held out her hand in greeting. After a moment's hesitation, Sasha shook her hand. The woman's fingernails were perfectly manicured while hers hadn't seen polish in months.

"The attorneys are on their way from the courthouse and should arrive within the hour."

Sasha nodded and was careful not to examine the

slight brown at the woman's perfectly blond roots. Instantly, she compared the woman's expertly applied makeup to the female sable's instinctual urge to groom before coming into season. The human animal had never been the subject of her academic studies, but she couldn't help but see the similarities with her professional research.

"Please follow me."

She stopped in a separate room. Three walls were covered in Impressionist art and the third wall was in fact a window looking out over the city.

"Please feel free to use the laptop, watch TV or peruse the magazines while you wait."

"Thank you."

"Can I get you something to drink, Ms. Clayton? Coffee, tea or soda?" she asked through a toothy smile that shouted cosmetic dentistry. The assistant kept addressing Sasha by her last name, a fact that made her feel older than her thirty-one years. She opened her mouth to tell the woman who had her beat in age by at least half a decade, that her name was Sasha. But she shoved the irritated thought to the back of her mind and she recalled the Southern tradition of calling adults by their last name.

"No, thank you." She smiled. "With the time change I won't have any trouble staying awake. It's the sleeping that will be difficult tonight."

"How about a mineral water? Transcontinental flights have a nasty tendency to cause dehydration. My skin is always parched even after a short flight to New York."

Startled, Sasha looked from the sight of the airplane flying in the horizon to Gretchen. "How did you know?"

"I made your travel arrangements. I hope that the flight and your hotel are adequate?"

"Very nice."

"Good. I'll go get that Pellegrino. Is there anything else I can get for you?"

"No, thank you," she responded with a hastily contrived smile. At that moment she was about to take anything to get the secretary away from her. Sasha watched the woman leave the room and sat in the stuffed leather chairs near the window. Needing something to grab a hold of besides her purse, she picked up a copy of the local newspaper and sat it on her lap.

She closed her eyes and sighed heavily. She thought she'd conquered her issues with being around people. Or she thought she had. Taking a hard look at her life for the past two years, she brutally came to the conclusion she was deluding herself. She hadn't spent more than a total of three months in civilization since she'd broken up with Byron Jackson.

They'd covered half of the Oregon wilderness and some of Washington. They'd slept in the same tent, splashed naked in the small mountain springs and tracked a den of migrating elk. It had been about this time of the year that he'd left her for a lucrative position as a college professor and a San Francisco socialite.

Sasha opened her eyes at the stab of pain in her stomach. The day after the break-up, she'd packed her bags and jumped on a plane to Cuba to visit her parents for two week. That's all she'd thought she'd need to get over the man she'd thought would be her life partner. Just a few days on the beach with her parents and she'd be back to her old self.

At least that what she'd told herself, until she'd returned to Oregon and walked past the campsite they'd stayed at weeks before. For months afterwards, she'd munched on antacids like they were peanuts and blamed it on a combination of stomach upset and food allergies. A quick trip to a village doctor in Vietnam had confirmed the fact that she had indeed been healing from a broken heart.

It wasn't that he'd found someone else. It really wasn't about Byron at all. She'd had this hope that she'd found her other half. Found the ideal relationship that her parents held. Someone who'd shared her love of animals, who understood her passion for natural research. She looked out over the wispy clouds towards downtown Atlanta and past the tall building to the skyline.

The sound of footsteps drew Sasha out of her thoughts. A glass and the signature green of the sparkling water sat on the side table next to her chair.

"Good Lord," she muttered. "I am such a selfish wretch. Here I am at the reading of Uncle Camden's will and all I can think about is my disastrous personal life."

"I suck," Sasha declared borrowing the phrase from one of the numerous in-flight movies she'd been forced to watch. She leaned her head back against the headrest and closed her eyes only to open them at the sound of someone entering the room.

"Yeah, that works. Pick out something nice with orchids. Yeah, have the note read, To my favorite ski bunny, have a wonderful birthday. Can't wait to see you on the slopes. Yes…yes…add the Belgian chocolate and something impressive. You know the kind— engraved and from Tiffany's. Good…Good… I'll call you later—got to take another call."

There was a brief silence and then the masculine voice continued. "Hey, little bit, sorry I missed your performance last night. You got the flowers, right? I'm sure that you've got a small greenhouse in that loft of yours. The New York dance scene will never be the same since you hit the stage. Of course, I'll be in the front row when the company comes to Atlanta. Good. I'll talk to you later okay? And congratulations."

In the silence, Sasha opened her eyes and thought about alerting the stranger to her presence. What a dog, she thought, and then revised her observation. Calling the man a dog was not only clichéd, but also a mistake in classification. The canine species had genetic pre- disposition for loyalty to their pack leader. Moreover, wolves were discerning in their choice of a mate. She stared down at the front page of the newspaper as if all the normal bad news had somehow become new and interesting on reading the paper. More uncomfortable than the time she'd overheard her parents making out in the laundry room, Sasha crossed her legs and loudly unfolded the newspaper in her lap.

She didn't look up or sideways and thus had an eagle eye of shiny black leather shoes on the plush Persian rug. Mr. Cell Phone settled in the seat next to hers.

"Sorry about that. I didn't see you over here," he said.

From across the room, Mr. Cell Phone's voice had only served to grate her nerves. Now less than five inches from her side, goose bumps prickled her flesh. The masculine tenor of his voice touched the primitive part of her psyche that she couldn't control.

Several seconds passed before Mr. Cell Phone crossed his ankle over his knee and Sasha heard the rustle of the leather as he sank back into the seat. "Looks like it's just us this afternoon, huh?"

She didn't respond but lifted her head and planned to give him a blistery cold stare. Instead, she blinked owlishly at what she observed had to be the cutest combination of smiling brown eyes and twin dimples that she'd seen in her life. Her heart just about flatlined when he smiled and she caught a glimpse of his less than perfect but nicely white teeth. Her thoughts stuttered to a stop and Sasha hurriedly returned her attention to the newspaper in the hopes that he would leave her alone.

She stared down at the black and white letters and

for the first time in her life cursed her gift of having a good memory. There was something irresistibly sexy about the stranger with the light boyish eyes. The man was handsome. Not the kind of cosmetically engineered, constant visits to the dermatologist, but the homegrown kind of good looking that came from a severe lack of ugliness in the recessive gene pool. His black curly hair was nicely cut and the clean-shaven look fit with his full lips.

"Mind if I grab the sports section? I haven't had time to catch up on the Falcons."

She almost retorted that was because he seemed to be busy juggling women, but she bit her tongue, pulled out the section and handed it over all without glancing in his direction.

"Thank you."

"Here's a glass of ice for your water, Ms. Clayton." Without asking, the secretary opened the bottle and poured the sparkling water into the glass.

"Thank you."

"Anything I can get for you, Trey?"

"I'm good."

Sasha bit the inside of her lip as Mr. Cell Phone got a name. But a sting of irritation prickled on her skin. The last thing she wanted floating around in her subconscious was the man's face, much less now that she could put a name to the person sitting at her side. Automatically, her hand reached out and she took a sip of the ice cold sparkling water. Tears sprang anew in her eyes and she began sniffing while she dug into her purse to pull out another tissue.

"Hey, it's going to be okay." He had the voice of an erotic dream. A hand touched her back and Sasha sprang up like a scalded cat.

"I'm not crying. It was the water."

"Sorry, again. Just wanted to help."

"I don't need your help," Sasha snapped out and instantly wanted to pull the words back. Normally, she wasn't rude. Then again she'd never had to deal with the set of circumstances she'd found herself in at that moment. Besides, she didn't know the man. And she didn't want to know him.

He stood up but made no move to come closer. Sasha's gaze slid from his black wool trousers over the tieless cobalt blue button-down shirt, past broad shoulders and a clean-shaven jaw to lock on to his full lips.

She swallowed hard.

"Look, Mrs. Clayton, what's the problem? I apologized."

Sasha used the irritation brought by his use of her last name to down the rising hormonal tide south of her waistband. "My name isn't Mrs. Clayton. That's my mother. I'm Sasha and just because we're in the same room doesn't mean I'm going to tell my life story to a stranger."

He stared at her like she had two heads and she glared back at him for having the nerve to look like the harmless boy next door when he was actually the wolf in the pasture.

"Okay let me try it this way. Sasha, what's the problem?"

"Nothing."

"Then can we clear up some of the hostility in the room? I'm not wearing my bulletproof vest today."

Sasha took his comment literally and asked, "Are you a police officer?"

"No, I'm a vet."

"A vet," she repeated doubtfully.

"As in veterinarian." He smiled in a way that crinkled his eyes and made her want to step forward. There was something magnetic. Something that reminded her of the pull of salmon swimming upstream. She witnessed the migration only once in her life but the sight of the hundreds of fish throwing themselves against the oncoming tides would forever remain in her memory as one of nature's truly inexplicable events. And all that wonder she felt looking into the man's eyes.

Trey continued. "I'm harmless and I love animals, so please, sit. I promise not to touch you. Not even if you were choking."

She relaxed slightly. "You don't have to go that far."

"Sure?" He chuckled. "Because we're in the office of one of the top law firms in the country and anyone of them can sue me for every dollar in the bank and the clothes on my back."

Sasha sat down and kept her hand on the hem of her skirt. The last thing she wanted to do was flash the man. She reached down and picked up the fallen newspaper.

"Can we start over, minus the rude phone conversation and the attempt to offer sympathy? I'm Trey Blackfox."

"Sasha Clayton."

He stared at her in a peculiar fashion for a moment, then seemed to shake it off. "Nice to meet you."

She smiled then looked back down at the paper. One inhaled breath brought the scent of cologne and, as if she'd stepping into a hot spring, every part of her body felt flush. It had to be his face. Something about the symmetrical features, masculine voice and pheromones that had her toying with the watch on her wrist instead of reading the words on the page.

She caught sight of him leaning in her direction. "Anything good in the news today?"

"Not unless robbery, apartment fires, another corporate bankruptcy and political scandals are counted as positive news items. Anything good in the sports world?"

"Nah, nothing happens until March Madness."

Sasha's brow slanted in a confused frown. "What's that?" Courtesy of growing up with globe-trotting parents and her continued work outside of the borders of the country of her birth and far away from cable television, it always took her months to get catch up on the latest phrases and trends.

"College basketball championships."

"Ahh." She nodded with understanding.

"Not into basketball?"

"I played center in college, and I've been to a few NBA games."

He gave her a quick onceover. "You've got the height. Something tells me you've got the skills."

"Don't put stock in that 'something' of yours. I sat on the bench eighty percent of the time. I liked the game. The game and the players just didn't like me. Did you play?"

"All the time. Caleb wouldn't let a weekend go by without pulling all of us into a game.

"All of us?"

"I have two brothers, a younger sister and a village of cousins."

"Sounds like a fun way to grow up."

"What about you?"

"Me?" Sasha replied while trying to discreetly scratch a spot on her stocking-covered leg.

"Any siblings?"

"No." She shook her head and, fearing ripping a hole in the only pair of stocking she owned, she flattened her hand and rubbed.

"Panty hose itching, huh?"

"Like the ten minutes after a mosquito bite."

"Yeah, it's a pain to wear stockings, especially on a hot summer day."

She looked at him suspiciously and her doubts about

his masculinity crept to the forefront of her thoughts. "And how would you know?"

Trey leaned a little farther into her personal space. "You can't just open up the book of my life and jump to the middle."

"*Autobiography of a Serial Dater* wouldn't be on my reading list anyway," she quipped.

He chuckled and the sound seemed to magically dissipate the knot that had formed in her stomach the minute she'd gotten in the chauffeured car that afternoon.

"No, this would be *The Trials and Tribulations of Being the Youngest Son.*"

"You don't look traumatized."

"It's the years of therapy."

Sasha took a sip of water and returned her attention to Trey's nice brown lips. Her eyebrow rose slightly as her lips curved into a smile. "Which kind? Shock or psychoanalysis?"

His legs spread out and their knees touched for a moment. Sasha almost spilled her drink as the brief contact sent a shiver throughout her body. It had been a long time since a man's touch had triggered such an instantaneous reaction. "It's more like mileage therapy."

"How does that work?"

"You put a minimum of a hundred miles between you and your closest relative. Only go back home on occasional weekends and move often so that your family can't find you when they want to drop in unannounced."

Sasha leaned back in her chair and covered her mouth with her hands. It took a second but the sounds that came out of her throat at first mimicked a croaking frog, but little by little, she opened her mouth and laughed. And the infectiousness of her laughter seemed to spread as Trey joined in the humor and it spread back and fourth until tears sprang into her eyes. She wiped them away and then looked over at him with new, friendlier eyes. "I needed that."

"Me, too. And I always get uncomfortable when I'm in the room with either a beautiful woman or a pet python."

"Even if a snake made it into the building, given the average fifty degree temperatures, it would have gone dormant the second it slithered into the ductwork. So I'm going to assume you were referring to me."

He lowered his gaze from her face and seemed to focus on her chest. Sasha fought the urge to fidget in her chair like a teenager on her first day at school.

"Before I clarify that statement, how did you know about a snake's body temperature?"

"The same way that I know that wolves in the wild and captivity practice a form monogamous pair bonds between the alpha male and alpha female, yet their domestic canine cousins have moved to the opposite end of the spectrum because of human interference and the lack of a pack family structure."

He gave her an incredulous look and just as he opened his mouth the executive assistant entered into the room. "Thank you for waiting, Ms. Clayton. Mr. Hawthorn will see you now."

Sasha stood and began to leave.

"Wait." Trey stood and blocked her path. His eyes ran up and down her body, letting Sasha know in no uncertain terms that Trey was interested in her in a physical way. "I'd like to finish this conversation."

"I think this place bills by the second." She smiled. "I need to go."

"What about dinner tonight?"

"Are you asking me out on a date?" she calmly questioned, although the palms of her hands had grown damp with the heady rush of excitement brought about by the unfeigned attraction from such a handsome man.

"Dinner at a nice restaurant and if we don't want the evening to end, coffee at my place." The way his eyelids lowered and those luscious lips curved upwards in a sexy suggestive grin kindled thoughts of sheets and pillows on the left side of her brain while the right side doused the effect by giving Sasha an instant playback of the conversation Trey was having when he'd entered the room earlier.

She stepped around him, then turned her head slightly to give him a sideways glace. She mustered a convincing indifferent tone. "Don't take it personally, but I don't date commitment-phobic bachelors." Then she walked away, moving from the waiting room as fast as low pumps would allow.

Five minutes later Trey was happy that he was sitting down, gleeful that he'd worn loose pants and downright grateful Sasha Clayton hadn't turned around as she'd left the room. He couldn't have turned his eyes away from the woman. Not even a myopic mole could have missed the hard outline of his groin. He shifted uncomfortably in his seat and when that didn't help, he put the newspaper over his lap.

Ten minutes. He had ten minutes to get the combination of Sasha's challenging stare and luscious rear end out of his head. Wide brown catlike eyes, rich hazelnut skin on an oval face. Not a perfect face like some of the models he'd dated in the past, but that mix of features and figure that men looked at and dreamed they woke up next to in the morning. Her dark hair looked as thought it was thick like his little sister Regan's. He wondered about the length. If the constrained tresses would curl at her shoulders or flow over her back. Trey ran a hand roughly across his close-shaven head.

He tried to think about Giselle, the painter and yoga instructor he'd let go three months ago. Her flexibility in bed had added an unexpected spice to their affair. Long slender face, crème caramel complexion and nice curves made a man drop to his knees in prayer, and she would show up at his door with just a phone call. And he could have easily flipped open his cell phone and called her up. However, the problem was he just realized that one glance from Sasha Clayton left him burning hotter than ten nights with *any* woman of his acquaintance.

Trey sat back in the chair and rubbed his brow as a full grin drew his lips upward. She was opinionated, touchy, feisty, cute and funny. And she'd turned him down. Trey Blackfox, son of one of Georgia's wealthiest African-American families, head of his own veterinary practice and millionaire bachelor got blown off.

"Trey?"

He looked up to see Gretchen's wary expression. "Sorry."

"Mr. Payton will see you now."

He stood but his mind remained fixated on the image of Sasha Clayton's perfectly sized backside. It took him twenty paces to get his libido in check and his mind on business. When he exited the waiting area, at least he had his common sense back.

Chapter 3

Sasha's pen hit the table at the same time her bottom lip dropped. "Excuse me, Mr…" Sasha blinked owlishly at the attorney. She sat at the head of a long conference table. A half dozen lawyers faced her. The first shock of the meeting was discovering that Uncle Camden had been cremated and his ashes spread over the Atlantic Ocean.

"Greenberg." The lanky gentleman with deep-set blue eyes and wispy silver hair responded.

"Could you repeat what you just said?"

"Save for a sum of a three million dollars bequeathed to various charitable trusts, two million to his trusted friend and butler, funds set aside for the progeny of his animals, the balance of Camden Ridgestone's thirty-five-million-dollar estate is yours with a few stipulations, of course."

Fully aware of the six sets of eyes on her, Sasha slumped in the leather armchair and struggled to keep her breakfast of eggs and croissants from rising up and spilling onto the nicely polished table.

"Are you alright?" another attorney asked.

She shook her head from side to side and honestly replied. "No."

"Don't worry. The stipulations are quite simple. You are to take on the duty of caring for the animals, take his seat on a few of the charity beards and you cannot give the fortune away."

Twenty-five million dollars. The amount swam in front of her eyes as she struggled to comprehend two things. First, how did Uncle Camden have that kind of money? Second, why in the world did he leave it to her? She'd spent half of her life believing that her godfather was a normal researcher with a British accent. It was only after her father and godfather had fought that she had discovered that there had been a lot more to Camden Ridgestone than they'd ever known. Like the fact that his well-to-do family had not completely disowned him. And that Camden had secretly funded her parents' research expeditions and Sasha's college education.

"I can see that this comes as a shock."

Sasha barely suppressed the urge to glare at the

white-haired attorney who'd long since given up on covering his receding hairline. The man had a gift for understatements. A hundred questions rose to her lips but Sasha settled on one. "Why?"

"Why?" Mr. Greenberg repeated with a puzzled look.

"Why me?" she croaked.

"Oh, that. Well, there are numerous reasons that are not my place to explain." He opened a leather portfolio and drew out a sealed envelope. "Camden left you this letter and I believe that it will provide you with answers."

The attorney slid it across the table in her direction, and then stood along with his colleagues. "We're just going to give you some time to take this all in. If you need anything, just pick up the phone and one of the secretaries would be happy to help."

"Thank you."

"There will be paperwork to sign. The main thing is that you begin your role as caretaker to Camden's animals. With your permission, I can have someone deliver your things from the hotel to the house."

"No, thank you. I can do it myself," Sasha replied as her head began to ache.

When the door closed behind them, she reached over and picked up the envelope, gingerly as if she held a rare specimen. With the corner of her fingernail, she flipped up the unsealed edge and drew out the thick pieces of off-white parchment.

Dearest Sasha,

Her heart gave a squeeze and fresh hot tears flooded into her eyes. Sasha closed the lids and drew in a deep calming breath. She wiped the tears away and forced herself to continue reading.

Don't panic, and remember to breathe. I've always been curious about your incredible dislike of surprises and I'm sure this bequest will be unexpected. But it is for the best. Of all the people in the world I trust, you, your father and your mother are highest on my list. And of all the people that I have loved, you, Sasha, deserve all the riches of the world although you've never wanted them. I leave this life without a child or close relatives. I've given my life to nature conservation and I've tried to be a good person. Now I hope that you will do the same. I leave you the bulk of my possessions. Do with the money what you will, but take care of my animals. All of them have kept me company and given me unconditional love. I could do no less than to leave them in your more than capable hands.

By the time she finished the letter, Sasha's hands shook. The enormity of the situation hit home as the missive landed on the table. From one hour to the next, she'd become a heiress and a pet owner. She didn't know which was worse. Her father had taught her to despise the rich. And despite her love of animals, she'd never owned a pet. She'd moved around too much during her childhood.

She looked down at the list and did a quick sum. She was now in possession of a fortune, a dog, cat, an iguana and a pod of tree frogs.

"Just checking in." Mr. Greenberg stood next to the table.

She opened her eyes and stood. "How long have I been here?"

"A little over half an hour."

She shifted in her seat as the attorney sat in the chair next to hers. Sasha wasn't physically tired but mentally she stood on the edge of exhaustion. "I'm sorry."

"No problem at all, young lady. Did you have a quick rest?"

"I didn't sleep. My head is still spinning."

"Well there's no rush. You have a lot to take in. It's not every day you inherit millions."

"What about Uncle Camden's family? Aren't they going to argue against this?"

"It's been taken care of. Your godfather is the poorest member of the Ridgestones and since he cut ties after moving to the U.S. and giving up his British citizenship, they're not going to say a word."

"Pardon my ignorance, but how did Uncle Camden amass this fortune?"

"Pet food."

"Excuse me?"

"Your uncle helped span a small dynasty of high quality, veterinary recommended pet food."

"I knew he had money, but this…" She shook her head. "I have no idea what to do now."

"You've got plenty of time to figure this out. And until you're ready to take control, our firm will continue to monitor the estate. The only thing that needs to happen now is that you move into the mansion. He was pretty adamant that you become the primary caretaker of the pets."

Sasha felt a momentary sense of panic. She'd helped rehabilitate injured wildlife and reintroduced them back into their natural environment, and tracked a pack of hyenas over the African plains. But she'd never taken responsibility of anyone or anything but herself.

"Now, don't panic."

She shook her head. "How did you know?"

"I can't read minds but I've seen that look on too many of my clients' faces not to recognize it. Camden has taken care of everything. In fact, another partner has just finished briefing someone who will be an integral part of your getting settled into your role. Just let me go get him."

Niggling in the back of her mind grew so that minutes later when the attorney entered the room she was numb to the surprise of seeing Trey Blackfox's familiar profile.

"Sasha Clayton meet…"

"Trey," she interrupted.

"You've met?"

"In the waiting room," Trey answered after walking in, pulling back a chair and making himself at home.

Sasha bit the inside of her cheek. The man was the epitome of confidence. And for a moment Sasha felt green with envy. Throw her into a room with a biologist, a den of wild aardvarks or a convicted felon and she could fend for herself. But being in a room with an attractive man left her tongue tied.

"Good. This should make this go a bit smoother. Trey and his veterinary clinic have been retained by the estate to continue in the primary capacity as both the medical care provider of the animals and advice for you."

She recovered her wits. "Shouldn't that be my decision? Not that I doubt his expertise."

"Normally that would be the case, but Mr. Ridgestone specified that the clinic not only care for the animals but he also provided a generous grant to ensure that they continue to receive the best care. Not to mention that since the clinic is nonprofit and gives free care, your uncle wanted to continue his support after his passing."

Trey chimed in. "In fact we're naming a new exercise run after your godfather."

She stared blankly at the two smiling men. Too much, too fast. She'd barely had a chance to adjust to the reality of her godfather's death. Now she had to deal with an inheritance that was incomprehensible in terms of her responsibilities. "I'm sure that you want to talk about this, but to be honest I can't think straight right now."

The attorney waved his hand. "You don't have to do anything. We'll be right here when you're ready to make any actions. My assistant reserved your hotel suite until tomorrow. Jackson has assured us that the house is ready for you."

"I'm not sure I feel comfortable moving into my uncle's house," she admitted.

"I understand, but part of the bequest entails you're being the animals primary caregiver."

Uncaring of the extra pair of interested ears that followed their conversation, Sasha made one last attempt to put the brakes on the increasing lack of control she had over the situation. "Not today. I don't think I can handle anything else."

The attorney nodded. "The car that picked you up this afternoon will take you back to the hotel." He stood and gave her another benevolent smile. "Tomorrow, I'll send someone by the house with the documents that I'll need you to review and sign."

Sasha slumped down farther in her seat.

"I'm sorry about your godfather. He was a good man."

Sasha swung her gaze from the attorney's retreating shoulders to Trey's solemn face. "I wish I'd know that he was sick. I would have been here."

"That would have been the last thing we would have wanted."

"Did you know that he was dying?"

"Not until I got a call from the hospital. He asked me to continue taking care of his animals and to help you in any way I could after he was gone."

"I take it that you're involved with the foundations the attorney mentioned."

"Yes. So it looks like we'll be seeing a lot of each other."

"It would seem so."

"About what happened in the waiting room," he started and stopped.

It took her a moment to notice his body language, but she suddenly realized that Trey felt uncomfortable in her presence.

She leaned close, cradled her face in her hands, and gave him a droll stare. "Please, tell me about what happened in the waiting room."

Trey swallowed. Odds were that the woman across the table wouldn't fall for the ole sweet charm that he'd been practicing ever since he'd graduated from Pampers to training pants. He'd tried a full smile and the compliments, but he'd gotten tackled before he reached the end zone. Now what did he do? He racked his brain for a quick solution to get himself out of the hole he'd inadvertently dug himself in by coming on to the woman who would be holding the purse strings to the grant money his clinic depended on. The fact that Camden had asked for him to assist his goddaughter was no small favor. Trey wouldn't betray that kind of trust just because his urge to peel the panty hose from Sasha's wonderfully formed legs. If he'd been thinking with his head instead of his libido, he would have realized that Sasha was Camden's goddaughter. He turned his mind back to the present. "I apologize."

Her face registered surprise at this apology. "For?"

He swore internally; she seemed determined not to make it easy. He placed his hands palms up on the conference table as he considered some way to make their predicament work. "My behavior in the waiting room. I have a tendency to go after what I want. Guess dealing with animal patients has rubbed on me. But, I don't want you to feel uncomfortable so I promise that I will follow your lead and keep our relationship strictly professional."

"You're either not in the habit of apologizing or you're not used to allowing someone else the upper hand."

He gave her a sheepish smile. "Does it show?"

"Like swarm of lightning bugs on a hot July night."

Her look changed from distant to one of warm humor. Her dark eyes sparkled with laughter as Trey leaned closer. That look with her lips upturned and mouth partially open made his fingers itch to touch her face. Made his lips long to taste hers.

Trey swallowed. "Guess I'll have to work on it. In the meantime, I'll expect to see Darwin for his checkup in the next two days."

"Of course." Sasha stood up from her chair.

Trey stood, came around the table, and stopped by her side. He reached into his wallet and pulled out a business card. "If you need anything, don't hesitate to call me."

"Thank you."

Before he could say anything else, Sasha turned and strolled out of the office. Lionel Ritchie's song "Two Times A Lady" rolled in his head as he watched her legs. Trey rubbed his brow and grinned. Life just kept getting interesting.

Two days after getting on a transcontinental flight, four hours since finding out that she'd become an instant millionaire and thirty minutes after leaving the law office, Sasha gasped aloud as the car pulled into a circular brick driveway. The seat belt sat forgotten in her hand as she took in the marble fountain, trimmed hedges and pristine lawn.

Sasha slowly exited the back of the luxury sedan with her mouth agape to greet her final shock of the day. "Uncle Camden lived here?"

The English Tudor seemed to come out of a Beatrix Potter novel. The brown-brick style open windows, nine-foot doors and exquisite masonry set it apart from all else. The home—no, she shook her head—the mansion would have fit perfectly in the North Lake District of England.

"Yes, ma'am."

Sasha's attention shifted and her mouth closed as she

focused on Jackson's response. "Let's make a deal. How about you never call me *miss* or *ma'am* and I won't call you Jeeves?"

She watched as his bushy eyebrows rose and his brows jumped from flat to deep crested waves.

"As you wish," he replied and then turned away to open the trunk.

Sasha stared at his back and half of her wanted to give up and scream. The other half ached to run for the nearest airport. However, she took a third option and surprised herself.

"As I wish?" She took a step closer and jabbed the man's shoulder with her outstretched finger. "As I wish?" Her voice rose slightly. "If I could I'd be back on the Malay Peninsula observing tapirs foraging for food. I'd have my uncle back." Tears popped out of her eyes. "That's what I wish." She sniffed. "And since I can't have that, I'd just like to have a tissue, please."

His expression softened and from out of nowhere a handkerchief appeared in Jackson's hand. "I apologize. Camden's loss has affected me more than I realized."

"I didn't even know that Uncle Camden was a millionaire. Sure as heck never dreamed that he'd leave this to me."

"I know that Miss—Sasha. He told me of his plans months ago."

"If that's true, then why the attitude?"

"Because every creature in that house, the future of the foundation in Camden's name depends on you. And for those pets to be properly cared for, you need to be here and not on the next flight to Singapore."

The tide of anger, which had a few moments ago rushed in, rushed out just as quickly. "You overheard my conversation with the attorneys?"

Jackson's look of offence couldn't be mistaken. "I assure you that I've been called many things, but an eavesdropper has never been one of them." He paused. "Your tickets were delivered to the hotel. I picked them up at the front desk."

Sasha looked down at the driveway then back to Jackson. She'd been on the receiving end of so many apologies that day that she'd lost count. "I'm sorry."

"Apology accepted. Now I think we can continue our conversation inside. It's a might bit nippy out here."

As they crossed the threshold, Sasha opened her mouth to ask another question, but something big and furry rubbed against her leg. She looked down to see the high-flung tail and the wide body of a long-haired-crème-colored cat as it pranced out of the room. She watched as a small dog with a leash in its mouth trotted slowly past her and dropped the leash at Jackson's feet. "Looks like someone needs a walk. If you'll excuse me."

The man left her standing alone under a two-story entrance foyer hung with a crystal chandelier that could have been plucked out of Buckingham Palace. While she tried to take some of the day's events in, the glasses of iced tea she'd drunk at lunch hit her bladder less than

a heartbeat later. All previous issues disappeared. Sasha
did a complete 360-degree turn and her eyes sought the
cat as it lay curled up on a carpet. "Know where the
bathroom is?"

Chapter 4

"I love you more, hummingbird," she repeated once again before hearing the tattletale click on the other end of the line. Barbara Clayton hung up the phone and walked outside the three-bedroom cottage she'd called home for the past decade. Her first instinct was to find her husband and tell him about Sasha's phone call. But her second thoughts won out. Turning left, she exited the walled garden and started down the worn path that would take her to the beach.

Memories rode the wind. She recalled their university days. When Camden, Arthur and she had long talks in the university library about migratory birds and human encroachment on the national forests. Always short on money, and big on ideas, they'd talked about saving animals. Barbara sat on a flat rock, curled her legs up, and hugged them to her chest. Resting her head atop her knees she stared at the ocean as the salty twang brushed across her cheeks. Minutes or hours passed as she sat immersed in her memories until a shadow crossed her face.

"Hey, sweetheart, I looked for you in the house and I thought you might be here. What's got that faraway expression on your eyes?"

"I was thinking about Camden." She shook her head slowly. "I still can't believe he'd dead."

Her husband was silent for several moments. "I know." He sat down, put his arm around her shoulders, and pulled her close. Even after over three decades of marriage, they still fit. She'd gained inches, he'd lost hair and they'd both lost sleep worrying about their work and daughter. But despite the ups and downs, she still felt that marrying him was the best thing she'd ever done.

Barbara laid her head on his shoulder and looked out over the sea. The waves continued to rise and fall, providing a semblance of something constant in a world of change. "Why did things have to end so badly?"

"Camden lied to us, butterfly."

She smiled softly at his pet name for her. She studied birds and he studied bats, yet they both shared a passion for butterflies. "But I could forgive him that."

"I could forgive a man for hiding the truth, but you can't help wonder what else he'd hidden."

"He was a good man."

"Who did an excellent job of fooling us into thinking he was a run-of-the-mill British man bent on making up for his country's past. But to find out that he's from one of those wealthy families that were actually responsible for all the natural damage that we're struggling to make right. It turns my stomach."

"You can't help what family you're born into."

"I made him my daughter's godfather. He was a member of our family and he was keeping secrets. Now when I go to give a lecture, or I'm offered a position at a university, I question whether it's because of my qualifications or Camden's influence. Not to mention I can't get over the fact that he funded Sasha's scholarship and fellowship."

She closed her eyes. Secrets. She still held one from her husband and if she didn't tell him about Sasha's being included in Camden's will she'd have another secret.

Maybe when he calmed down.

She watched the waves knowing Miami was ninety miles in the distance. Her husband crossed his arms over his chest and stared toward the water. "Money is the root of evil. History has shown us that. Never doubt it. I'm just glad none of this ever touched Sasha."

Barbara looked away and kept her mouth closed.

Chapter 5

The next morning the first thing Sasha did was to pick up the mobile phone and head into the large guest suite bathroom. "Lena, are you awake?"

"Would I answer the phone if I wasn't?"

"Sorry to call you so early."

"No, no, I need to get my lazy butt out of bed and head to the library."

"How are things?" Although they only saw each two or three times a year, Sasha so valued Lena's friendship that she'd dropped over a thousand dollars on a plane ticket and flown for over eighteen hours to attend Lena's New York engagement party earlier in the year. Half-sick with a stomach virus, she'd thrown up on Noah, her best friend's fiancé. Luckily, the dentist lived close by.

"Mom and Noah are pushing for a wedding date. My future mother-in-law is campaigning for a baby. Dad's taking Viagra and my older sister Kelly's driving me nuts with some crazy diet she just started. Something about only eating foods that start with certain letters of the alphabet on certain days of the week. I can't keep people from bothering me long enough to finish the outline for my thesis. My blood pressure is high. Might get a weave because my hair is split, broke and shot to hell. Did I mention my pregnancy scare last month? And I went to the emergency room with a panic attack. How about you?"

"Good. Great," she lied.

"Where are you?" Lena asked. "I'm hearing a serious echo. Are you in some third world country? Do I need to call the UN to get you out?"

"My godfather left me twenty-five million dollars, a mansion and his pets. I'm calling from the guest bathroom."

"You're kidding?"

"No, I'm not."

"You don't seem too happy about it. I'd be over the moon. Not about your godfather dying, but about the inheritance."

"This is a huge life changing responsibility."

"Bump that. This is a once in a lifetime chance for

a shopping spree. Book a ticket and I'll pick you up at the airport."

"It's not my money."

"Not according to your uncle's will."

"Lena," Sasha softly chided.

"Girl, you've just won the lottery and you're acting like somebody died."

Her lips turned down. "Someone did."

"I'm sorry—you know I didn't mean it that way."

"I know. It's just this is really unsettling. The house is big enough for a village and I can't imagine how to manage this money, the animals, not to mention managing the foundation."

"You know you've always had money issues."

"I've never bounced a check."

"Not those kinds of money issues. I mean you just don't like money."

"Are you surprised? My parents started out as socialists before they moved to Cuba."

"Look, why don't you put the life crisis on hold and catch the first non-stop flight to New York?"

Sasha nibbled on the inside of her lip for a second. "I can't. I've got the animals to look after."

"You've got millions. Hire the Nanny. Heck, you can probably get the Crocodile Hunter."

"Uncle Camden's last wish was for me to take care of this, Lena. Although I would love to pack a bag and go, I just can't."

"I understand."

She thought about it for a moment. "But, I was thinking since I can't leave how about you come here? I've got plenty of space and you sound like you could use a break."

"Keep that option open. If that fiancé of mine pulls out one more wedding book, I'll be knocking on your door."

She rested her chin in the palm of her free hand. "I just want to get rid of the money, but I can't because of a clause in the will."

"Wait. I'm sorry, I think there must have been some static in the line. I thought I heard you say that you wanted to get rid of twenty-five million dollars."

"I do," she replied.

"You're crazy."

"No, I'm simple. I take what I need. No more, no less. My father taught me that."

"Come on, Sasha," Lena returned. "It's not that bad. What can you complain about now? You're rich."

"What about my career? I'll have to cancel all of my planned expeditions. For the unforeseen future, I have to meet with attorneys on a weekly basis, I have an appointment with the vet this morning because the dog isn't eating, I need to meet with the household staff, figure out what charity board meetings to go to and the list keeps growing. Truly this is a good example of more money, more problems."

There was a knock at the door. "Sasha, just a reminder that Darwin needs to be at the vet in an hour."

"Who was that?" Lena loudly questioned.

"Jackson."

"And who is Jackson?"

"The butler."

"Oh my God! I bet you have a maid."

"I think so," she confessed or hoped. The idea of Jackson cleaning up her bedroom and making her bed made her uncomfortable. "I haven't met anyone yet, but Jackson says he'll introduce me to the cook later on today."

"Promise me you'll call me after nine o'clock tonight. I'm running low on my daytime minutes."

She smiled. "Promise."

"Take care."

"You, too."

She hit the End button and placed the phone on the marble vanity. Sasha's eyes landed on the cat lying atop one of the bathroom's plush bath rugs. Zaza, the ex-homeless Persian that now dined on high-end cat food and pooped in a custom kitty litter pan. The cat was simple enough to take care of but, God forbid if the cat got pregnant. According to the terms of Uncle Camden's will Zaza's kitten would end up with an inheritance of about twenty thousand dollars apiece. Sasha sunk down on the toilet as the weight of it all felt like an anchor on her shoulders. How could she find good homes for them? She didn't know anyone who lived in a stable enough environment to raise a cat. All of her girlfriends were over thirty and vowed never to be crazy single cat women.

She stood and glanced at her reflection in the mirror. Her hair was still a natural mess, her eyebrows had long since gone wild and her fingernails still needed attention. Her feminine pride balked at seeing Trey again.

After digging through her suitcase for ten minutes, Sasha pulled out trousers and an ivory cable knit sweater. She put on lip gloss and pinched her cheeks.

An image of Mr. Cell Phone, a.k.a Trey Blackfox, rose in her mind as she released the necklace clasp. She stared at the teardrop opal her father had given her on her fifteenth birthday. The last thing she needed was another distraction in her life. It was way too complex already. She especially didn't need to waste time fantasizing about a man who couldn't commit to her. Moreover, if she were going to pick a man based on more than good looks and charm, Trey didn't measure up.

Later, after she'd had enough time to make her appearance halfway decent, Sasha walked downstairs and searched the house for her newest charge. She found Darwin lying at the foot of her godfather's bed. The sight if his head dropping down as soon as she'd opened the door about broke her heart in two.

The Jack Russell terrier didn't even look as she put on his leash and took him downstairs. Once they'd settled into the back of the car, Sasha caught Jackson's look of concern in the rearview mirror. Darwin had been her uncle Camden's constant companion. If her godfather flew first class, Darwin had his own seat.

She'd met the canine when both she and Uncle Camden had been in Brussels for a wildlife preservation symposium.

She reached down, picked up the dog and put him in her lap and held him. It was almost as if she were holding piece of her godfather. She'd always known he'd loved animals, but she'd never visited his house, or met any of his other pets. She'd been aware of them only from letters. Yet in the back of her mind there had always been the expectation that she'd one day visit the house and meet the little creatures in person.

Sasha looked down and stroked the fur on the dog's head. "Oh, Darwin. I know how you feel. I miss Camden, too, tough guy."

His face lifted up and his dog tag jiggled back and forth twice and that brought a smile to her face. "Yes, I called you tough guy." She used the nickname that her godfather had given the canine.

Minutes later with Darwin in her arms, Sasha carefully made her way across the parking lot and stopped in front of the automatic glass doors of the clinic. As they opened to reveal a large reception area, she had to blink as her eyes adjusted from the bright sunlight of the interior of the office. She glanced from left to right and would have backed out had she not seen the name of the office: Samuel Graham Veterinary Clinic. Stepping through the reception area she walked toward the smiling young man seated behind the counter.

"Good afternoon. I'm here to bring…" she started.

The young man smiled and reached over to rub Darwin's head. "Little D, I haven't seen you in ages."

Sasha blinked as the Jack Russell terrier in her arms seemingly went from death to life; Darwin practically jumped from her arms into the assistant's. She looked at his nametag: Joseph Morris.

"Oops. Sorry about that." Sasha stepped forward in an attempt to reclaim the canine.

"I've given him special treats since he was weaned." He chuckled, struggling to keep his face from the dog's tongue. "How are you doing, fella? Looks like you've lost quite a bit of weight."

"Yes, that's what I'd like to speak to a doctor about."

"Of course, Ms. Clayton."

She gave the young man a warm open smile she normally reserved for animals and kids. "Please, call me Sasha."

"Only if you call me Jo." He grinned broadly. "Sasha, I'm Dr. Blackfox's veterinary assistant and I'll he helping with Darwin today. Now, if you'll just have a seat, I'll take you back as soon as a room becomes available."

Sasha took the dog from his arms and settled into one of the comfortable waiting chairs. "So you like treats, boy? I'll have to buy you a box before I leave."

Leave. The word left an uncomfortable taste in her mouth. She'd only arrived in Atlanta yesterday and already her mind was mentally preparing to depart. "Poor pooch. It must seem like everyone is leaving you," she murmured.

Her eyes strayed to the other people with their pets and she felt a momentary pang of envy. Although she studied animals for weeks or months at a time, she could never bond with them the way those people had bonded with their pets. Her parents had moved around so much that having a pet was never an option. Once she'd tried to befriend one of her mother's wounded birds, but having an endangered hawk as a pet was against the law.

She thought of her parents and her heart sank. She'd have to tell them. There was no way she could deliver the news on the phone. She'd have to fly to Cuba and do it in person. She shook her head and rubbed Darwin's back. *One step at a time, Sasha,* she told herself. Now if she could get through seeing Dr. Trey Blackfox as easily.

Chapter 6

Rosalind Blackfox took a seat in the plush waiting room chair. Her eyes looked over the room with satisfaction. She'd worked hard to make sure the interior designer created an area that resembled more of a doctor's waiting room than a veterinary clinic. The interior design firm she'd picked out for Trey had done an excellent job of making the room both comfortable and functional. A little furry head moved on her lap drawing her eyes downward. "You have to wait your turn like everybody else, Christmas." The little terrier laid his head back down on her leg and closed his eyes.

"He's adorable."

Rose looked at a woman sitting a seat away. Pretty,

but she would be stunning with a visit to the salon and touch of makeup. The woman's flawless complexion helped a lot. She glanced down at the stranger's left hand and noticed the absence of a wedding band. It only took the lack of a ring to set the matchmaking part of her mind to humming. She had three eligible sons and a single daughter and no grandchildren.

"My husband gave him to me for Christmas."

"He looks like a puppy."

"Actually, Christmas is two years old." Rose laughed as the younger woman's eye widened.

"He's what the breeders call a teacup. He's actually smaller than a toy terrier. What is yours?"

"Darwin is a Jack Russell terrier." Sasha paused. "I think he's about three years old."

"Adopted?"

"Inherited." She looked away. "Darwin was my godfather's companion."

"I'm sorry."

Sasha's lips trembled. "Thank you"

Alarmed, Rose pointed at the dog lying immobile on the floor. "Will he be alright?"

"I don't know. It seems that he's not eating and barely drinking. He won't leave Uncle Camden's room. I think that he's waiting for my godfather to come back."

"Poor thing. Which doctor will be seeing him?" Rose sent out a quick prayer to God that the answer was her son. She worried about all of her children, but Trey needed more attention than the others. At least Marius and Cable stayed close to home so she could keep an eye on them. Her daughter… Her daughter, Regan, was in the foreign service.

"Dr. Blackfox."

Rose looked away to hide the "cat that ate the canary" grin she knew was pasted on her face, then covered the act by stroking Christmas's head. "So are you from Atlanta?"

"I was born in Texas and I spent most of my high school years in between South Carolina and my parents' research expeditions."

"What do they do if you don't mind my asking?"

"My mother is a bird researcher and my father's a biologist who's specializing in bats at the moment."

Rose looked up at the ceiling and said to herself, "Thank you, Lord."

"So you've just moved here?" Rose asked out loud.

"My godfather lived here. He left me his pets and some other things in the will."

"Well, this city is lucky to have you. We need a few more Southerners."

"I'm not so sure. I'm also a researcher and I have a small studio in Brooklyn just to store my stuff and have place to crash when I'm back in the U.S. It's a little scary to think about having to stay in one place. I don't know anyone or know where to go. As you can see." She paused to point to her hair. "My hair hasn't seen a salon in months."

"Oh, no. It looks nice."

"Look, Mrs…"

"Call me Rose."

"Please call me Sasha. You are sweetheart, but let's be honest. My hair needs help."

"Sasha, what are you doing after this?"

She chewed on the thought for a little while. For the first time in her life, she didn't have a clue as to what she would do next. Sasha wound her finger around Darwin's leash. "Going back to a large empty house, I guess."

"No, we are having lunch and you can come with me to the salon. Fredrick will be thrilled to get his hands on you hair."

"What about Christmas and Darwin?"

"Trey can take good care of them while we're gone. They have an excellent kennel facility in the back."

Sasha looked tempted by the thought having someone else deal with her hair, and also looked forward to the opportunity to avoid thinking about things. "Well, I can have Jackson come back later to pick me up."

"Good. I'll just make a quick phone call and we can be on our way."

"Hey, Trey, your eleven o'clock is in the waiting room and, man, is she sweet."

Trey's brow wrinkled as he dropped the pen onto his desk. "Jo, are you feeling well today?"

"Of course, I had my protein shake for breakfast and I'm about to grab a granola to keep the energy up. Why? What's up?"

"Rigdestone's dog is male."

"Trey, I wasn't talking about the dog. I was talking the woman who brought him in. Maybe she's the girlfriend. Would be like that old British man to have a fashion model or something like that." He cocked his head to the side and grinned. "I can see him as an undercover playa being that this is the South. You know, kinda like Atlanta's Hugh Hefner? I can picture that rich man with a dozen women hanging around the mansion. She's a nice brown-skinned honey, too. I think she might like me."

"Right," he replied. Trey shook his head sadly. Another crush for Jo. Trey looked at digital clock on the wall of his office and one word popped into his mind: *Sasha.* He pushed back from his chair and stood. He took a moment to run a hand over the white doctor's coat and he spared a quick glance at the wall mirror. Not that he was a vain man, but he'd been taught since birth how to make a good impressions and seeing as how he and Sasha had gotten off on the wrong foot the first time they'd met, he wouldn't want to make the same mistake twice.

Jo continued to lean against the door dressed in sneakers and scrubs. "Oh, I almost forgot to tell you that your mother's here. Man, we're lucky because she dropped off three dozen boxes of gourmet cookies. All the girls are going nuts down there."

Trey froze like a cornered dog. Rosalind Blackfox, affectionately called Rose by everyone but her kids, didn't just stop by out of the blue. "What's she doing here?"

Jo's grin broadened. "She said something about shots for Christmas, but the last I saw she was in deep conversation with Sasha Clayton."

The thought of his mother talking to the object of his 2:00 a.m. fantasies made Trey fly out the door and down the hallway. Less than three minutes later when the elevator doors opened, the sight of Sasha laughing with his mother took his breath away. Trey wasn't sure if it was fear or some unknown affliction.

"Good morning, ladies—" he bent down and quickly patted Christmas and then stooped lower to pat Darwin on the head "—and gentleman."

"Trey Sinclair Blackfox, is that any way to greet your mother?"

"Hi, Mom." He leaned down and made sure that he stopped before squishing the little dog in her lap. It had taken months for Christmas to warm up to anyone other than his mother and father. Now was not the time to make enemies with his mother's fifth child.

"Much better. Trey, you must meet this nice young woman I just met. Sasha Clayton, this is my son Trey." His mother's eyes narrowed.

Sasha cleared her throat and managed to hide a smile at the panicked look on Trey's face. "We met the other day."

"I had no idea Rose was your mother." Sasha's mouth opened in a small O and Trey's eyes fastened on her lips. He'd seen plenty of movies where the director slowed the camera frames to emphasize the moment, but he'd never experienced slow motion in reality. Yet, now it seemed that time had slowed to a crawl. Sasha's tongue moved enticingly around her generous bottom lip.

She looked between them both. Trey could see the way her brain struggled to find similarities. Only if she compared the eyes would she find a match. The family had a long-standing joke that Marius, his oldest brother, might act like their grandfather, but Trey was the old man's spitting image.

"Don't worry," his mother said as her smile blossomed and her eyes twinkled with amusement. "He looks like his grandfather, so he'll be keeping his hair."

"Mom, what are you doing here?"

"Christmas needs his shots."

"Why didn't you go to the place back home I recommended? Caroline Jackson is the best vet in town."

"I wanted to check up on you."

"You drove an hour and a half to check up on me?" Trey asked with a grin.

His mother reached up and ran her fingertips through her hair. "Well I need to stop by the salon, and to do a little shopping. Your grandfather's birthday is in a few weeks. I need to pick up his watch from the jewelers."

In a hurry to separate his mother from Sasha, Trey

nodded nervously. "If you can wait for about a half hour, I'll take good care of Christmas, right after I see to Darwin here."

His mother's smile increased. "Oh, yes. And since there will be little chance of you joining me for lunch, I'm very luck that Sasha has agreed to come with me."

"Huh?" Trey croaked. He hadn't realized how much he wanted to keep his personal life separate from his family. He'd never introduced his mom to any of his girlfriends. "But what about us spending time together? We can go to this great bistro down the street."

His mother stood up and patted him on the shoulder. "We'll talk at dinner tonight. Now please call Jo so that I can make sure that Christmas is okay and you can see to little Darwin here. Make sure you're extra nice. I think that the little puppy needs some extra TLC."

Trey started to argue but the gleam in his mother's eye slapped him back to elementary school, and anything he was about to say froze in his throat. Rosalind Blackfox had raised three boys and tamed their dad. He'd learned early when he should give in. Trey's shoulders fell. "If it's okay I'll have Dr. Russell administer the shots."

"That lovely older gentleman you interned with?"

Trey nodded. "That's him."

"Good, good." She turned her attention to Sasha. "Don't worry, he'll give Christmas yummy treats, and I can find out what you've been up to for the past few months."

Trey shook his head. Ben Russell was one of the best

surgeons in the Southeast with an incredible affinity with animals. A proverbial man of few words, Ben measured out words as if they were money from his wallet.

"Ready to go back to the examination room?"

"Lead on." Sasha smiled. As they walked down the corridor, Sasha's heels clicked on the floor. She looked at Trey sideways. "I like your mother."

"Don't let her fool you. She's an amateur detective. Just open the door a crack and she'll get your life story."

She couldn't help but smile at the chagrin that crept into his voice. "I don't think so. This time I have a feeling that all she'll want to talk about is you."

"Don't believe a word because there's not a lot to know. I'm thirty-three years old, single, never married, two brothers, one sister, Georgia native and I'm a vet."

"That's it?"

"In a nutshell. What you see it what you get."

"Same here."

"Smart, pretty and loves animals. Can't beat that," he said.

A flush spread through Sasha. Despite her worldly travels, she'd never learned how to accept a compliment. Especially when she didn't feel as though she actually deserved it. "Why did you become a veterinarian and not a doctor?"

His face took in a thoughtful expression. "Not for the money or the prestige. I almost became a doctor, but my older brother got to med school before I did. So

I switched to something better. I chose veterinary medicine because I love and enjoy working with animals. What about you?"

She caught her lower lip with her teeth. He asked the right questions at the right time and he was sincere. Then there was his scent. Sometimes she wished that she wasn't so sensitive, but he smelled good, like the earth, with an underlying masculine scent that was very sensual. "Sasha?"

Trey was watching her face. Sasha forced herself to make eye contact. "Yes?"

"So is it a secret?"

She shook her head not so much in denial, but in confusion since she'd forgotten his question. "No."

"Then what exactly prompted you to become a wildlife researcher?"

She blinked. "I couldn't image doing anything else but following in my parents' footsteps."

His brow wrinkled. "What do your parents do, if you don't mind my asking?"

"Wildlife biologists."

Trey snapped his fingers, then stopped in the doorway of an examination room. "Now that you mention it, I remember Camden talked about your parents. He and your father were best friends and won acclaim for their research."

"You've got a good memory."

"I've got a lot of good things. So you enjoy your afternoon with my mother and try not to worry. You'll be leaving this guy in good hands."

Sasha leaned down and rubbed Darwin's head. His tail wagged a little, then stilled. She looked back up at Trey. "Thanks."

Six hours later Trey was once again in the examination room with Sasha. Only, this time it was going to kill him. Everything about her from the thick, below-the-ears hair with salon silkiness; the nails; glowing skin and enticing perfume. Not even bothering to look over from the computer monitor displaying the patient's vital statistics, Trey began the practiced speech he'd given over a thousand times since he'd opened the veterinary practice. "This morning I examined Darwin and don't worry he didn't..." His voice trailed off as his eyes trailed over a pair of per-fectly shaped calves to a black skirt, then drifted over curved breasts pushing out from under her blouse. She had a slender unadorned throat. His gaze stopped on her luscious lips.

"Trey?" she asked.

He shook his head a little and coughed to hide the fact that he'd completely lost his train of thought while his second head came to attention. "Apologies," he managed to get out after his coughing eased. Pulling himself together, he managed to look her in the eyes and instantly regretted it. Jo had been right on the money. This woman had it going on. "Allergies," he lied.

"Are you allergic to dogs?" she asked.

"Dust. I'd be in for a world of hurt if I were allergic to these guys." He laughed while taking a step closer to Sasha and the canine on the examination table. Against the sterile smell of the room, her scent almost knocked him down. She smelled feminine, sexy and sweet.

"You were saying that he didn't…"

"Feel any discomfort," Trey finished. Between one heartbeat and the next, he sent up a small prayer of gratitude that he wore a doctor's coat. Nothing short of elastic baggy sweatpants could have hidden his erection. He swallowed the urge to let lose a swear word or two. He hadn't had anything happen like this since he'd "accidentally" walked in on his sister's slumber party.

"So he's going to be okay?"

"Darwin's going to be fine." Trey's eyes moved from Sasha's face and settled on the hand absentmindedly stroking the Jack Russell's head. *Focus,* he told himself. He'd been in the examination room with hypochondriac owners who brought their dogs in every three weeks, socialite ex-wives on the prowl for husband number two, crying screaming kids and even an resentful husband who had tried to bribe him to kill his wife's toy Maltese. In each instance, he'd reacted with a calm professional demeanor. Yet, Sasha Clayton had him almost jumping out his skin with the urge to run his hands over her body and kiss her neck.

"Jackson says that he's lost weight."

"He just misses his owner. I'm going to take additional tests on Darwin but it looks like a very simple case of canine depression. This breed is known for the deep attachment they have toward their owners and their families."

"What can be done?"

"There's medication. A kind of canine Prozac or the more natural way would be to spend more time with him. He'll never forget his original owner but, perhaps you can pull him out this funk. In the meantime, I'd like to keep him overnight."

She paled. "Why?"

"Calm down," he soothed, placing a hand on her shoulder. "It looks like Darwin might be a little dehydrated. An intern will be here to check on him periodically through the night."

For a moment, Trey wanted to take back his request when he caught the sparkle of unshed tears in Sasha's eyes.

"Whatever you feel is best," she said, looking away.

Trey lightly brushed her chin with his fingertips to bring her eyes back to his. "I promise to take good care of him."

"I know." She sniffed and then wiped her eyes.

Under normal circumstances, Trey would have grabbed the dog and hit the door. He couldn't stand to see a woman cry. He could handle the kids, but not the parents. This time, however, he stepped close to Sasha, reached out and pulled her into his arms. He was not only surprised at how well she fit but also that her body shook.

"Come on. Let it out."

"I shouldn't be here. We shouldn't be here. How could he leave without saying goodbye? Why didn't he tell me? I should have known. I should have been here for him," she babbled.

"Maybe it's a male thing. We always think we're invincible. It's going to be okay."

"I'm sorry," she said, pulling back. "Now I've gotten makeup on your jacket."

"Don't worry about that. I've had a lot worse on this thing. Thank goodness for bleach, huh?"

She let out a small chuckle and the sound went straight to his heart.

"Dr. Blackfox."

"Trey," he corrected.

"Thank you."

"Save that for tomorrow if we've got this boy eating premium dog food and barking up a storm."

"Okay."

Sasha walked alongside Trey to the waiting room and turned toward him as they stood next to the reception station. Thinking about leaving reminded her that she should call the house. "Can I use your phone? I need to call Jackson and have him pick me up."

"No, you can't," he said, and then took off his white doctor's coat revealing dark heather slacks and a turtleneck.

It took a few seconds for his response to settle into Sasha's brain. "Why not?"

"My mother made me swear that I would drive you home."

"Don't you have work to do?"

He waved his hand around the empty reception area. "You were the last appointment."

"What about your mother?"

"We're having dinner tonight. I bet she and Christmas are halfway to the pet store."

"I don't want to inconvenience you. I mean we just met the other day."

"It's not only my pleasure, but also my job."

"I don't understand."

"About a year ago, your godfather walked in here, dropped off a quarter of a million dollar check, vowed to continue his support of the shelter and then adopted a cat. Now that you've taken over his estate, Sasha, you are my clinic's primary benefactress and if driving you home can return your generosity, then so be it."

"I'm not the one that deserves your thanks, Trey. It's not my doing."

A corner of Trey's mouth turned up. "True. But I can't show my appreciation to someone who's not here and your godfather did make a personal request that I look out for you."

Sasha raised her hands in mock defeat and he saw a tiny smile. "Okay, I give up."

"Good. You take a seat and I'll grab my keys, tell the staff I'm leaving and we'll be on our way."

Trey pivoted and strode down the hallway. Sasha looked at his back and butt. Unwrinkled wool slacks covered his legs and cupped the two defined cheeks. She quickly looked away before he turned the corner and caught her staring. Good Lord. She put a hand to her forehead and rubbed her brow. She'd been infatuated numerous times in her life, but she could tell this crush was shaping up to be a really bad one.

Driving alone in a car with Sasha wasn't going to be as easy as Trey thought. The SUV was huge. And the silent space, the scent of Sasha's perfume mixed with the new car smell, the vehicle seem all the more intimate.

When she'd asked him about the dashboard features, he'd tried to answer her questions and failed miserably. Somewhere in the oversize glove compartment he had a two-CD box set of instructions on how to operate all the luxury features that he'd added like the heated seats, surround sound, the navigational system and in-roof DVD player.

She stared at the dashboard, "It's a very nice car. Your practice must be doing well."

"I do okay." He shrugged. Complete lie. The clinic was barely in the black. Without supplement donations from private donors and infusions of cash from Trey's trust fund, it would have been out of business. Trey didn't even take a salary from the clinic.

"Turn right, then left. It's the house in the cul-de-sac."

For the first time since he'd pulled out of the parking lot, Trey paid attention to the residential area. The Vinings district of Atlanta was famous for its exclusive mix of nouveau riche and old money. As he pulled into the driveway of the house, Sasha pointed toward his wrinkled brow at the sight of the two-story mansion. He'd grown up around money and he had a good idea about how much things cost. The woman sitting in the passenger seat didn't seem like the type of woman who lived in a million-dollar mansion.

Trey stopped the car in the in front of the entrance-way and killed the engine. "This is your place?"

"No," she replied shaking her head. "The place is my godfather's. I pay rent on a small co-op in Brooklyn."

He took off his seatbelt. "I didn't peg you for the big-city type."

She shook her head and smiled. "I'm not. I hate cities. I only keep the place because it's near the airport and I need an address for my passport."

"Why not your parents' place?"

She chuckled before taking off her seat belt. "I don't think that would be possible since they moved to Cuba a few years ago."

"Oh."

She unbuckled her seat belt and paused before opening the door. "Would you like come inside and say hello to your other patients?"

"I'd love to. I haven't seen Zaza since Camden brought her in to get her teeth cleaned."

Sasha stared at him. "You clean a pet's teeth?"

"There's nothing like a little cavity prevention."

"I've been out of the country way too long." She laughed.

Trey stood behind her as she pulled out a key and unlocked the door. As soon as her foot touched the hardwood floors, ceiling lights illuminated the empty foyer. "Jackson?" Sasha called out. Second passed and there was no response. "That's strange. Who turned on the lights?"

Trey scanned the area and his eyes fell on a small infrared light. "I think it's automatic."

"Oh."

"I'm just curious, but who is Jackson?"

"Tall, older, British gentleman who worked for my godfather."

"Does he wear driving gloves and a tweed hat?"

"That's him." She smiled. "I guess he's not here."

"This is a *nice* house."

Sasha shook her head and resumed walking toward the wing of the mansion that housed the greenroom. It took her a few wrong turns, but she eventually led them into the glassed-in area that housed Uncle Camden's iguana and tree frogs. With the last rays of sunlight beaming through the windowed ceiling, the area took on a tropical ambiance. "It's too big. You could fit a Polynesian village in here and still have room."

Trey stepped into the room and let loose a low whistle. "I don't want to pry, but is this place is expensive to keep up? I knew Camden had deep pockets, but this is truly impressive."

Sasha clamped both hands together as the need to talk to someone about the inheritance beat like a herd full of elephants in her chest. "Trey, Uncle Camden left me twenty-five million dollars, the house, the animals and the responsibility of providing oversight for his foundation."

On the verge of hysterics, Sasha hugged herself. "All I wanted was to research animals in their natural habitat. Eventually I would settle down, get married, have a child and a cat and live in a normal house with a small car. Now I'm in this huge mansion and have responsibility for a dog, a cat, an iguana and a foundation."

She closed her eyes and then froze as she felt strong arms pulling her forward. Her brow rested on his broad shoulder and Sasha relaxed in Trey's embrace. "All I want is to have my godfather back so I can make him undo this mess."

Several heartbeats passed in silence before Trey spoke. "Everything will be alright, Sasha."

She kept her eyes closed and breathed deeply. The clean scent of his aftershave tantalized her nose. She sighed before answering, "My father practically excommunicated Uncle Camden from our lives after finding out he had money. He'll lose it when he finds out that I've inherited all of this."

"It can't be that bad."

"I wouldn't be too sure about that. Long before I was born my father added wealthy people and capitalism to his list of the seven deadly sins."

More reluctant than she'd dared admit, Sasha stepped out of his arms. "Part of me feels the same way."

"Sasha, I knew that Camden wasn't a pauper—after all, he did make generous donations to the shelter. But even I didn't know that he was a multimillionaire."

"You and me both." She weakly chuckled. "My god-father was a different breed of man. He was honorable, decent, kind, caring and fair."

"I agree. Having money doesn't make a person bad. It's what they do with their money that counts."

"You're right."

Trey cupped his ears. "What did you just say? I couldn't hear you."

Sasha laughed and the sound reached way down in his gut and relaxed muscles he didn't know were tensed.

She playfully swatted him on the shoulder. "Very funny."

Trey grinned thinking about how long it had been since he'd enjoyed himself so thoroughly. "I'm sorry, but I've had a complex since I was little. There has to be some unwritten rule in my family that no matter what the men say, the women will always tell them they're wrong."

"I can tell you know that I call a spade a spade and a snake a snake. When it comes to Uncle Camden's pets, you're the expert."

"You've got a deal. And when it comes to monkeys, aardvarks, elephants and anything else that belongs in the forest, I'll leave that up to you."

He reached out his hand with his palm upward with every intention of shaking her hand. But as soon as the warmth of her palm touched his, his fingers closed and all of Trey's senses were full of her. He savored the sight of her: her midnight hair gleaming in the setting sun, her flawless brown skin, her eyes—deep brown, like Georgia pine—the feel of her skin, soft as silk, yet suggestive of great strength and tremendous resilience in her touch; and her scent. Something sweet and soft, sandalwood, he thought, combined with the subtle scent of her own body in a blend that was heady enough to drown him. Trey drew a deep breath.

He lowered his head and settled his mouth on hers. He felt her initial resistance slowly melt away and he pulled her closer, deepening the kiss. When her lips parted and allowed his tongue entrance, the sweetness of it rocked his world.

Suddenly, Sasha pulled away and backed up. "That was unexpected," she said softly.

"Was it unpleasant?" he asked in a deep, husky voice. He didn't ask out of curiosity because Trey knew enough about women to know that Sasha had enjoyed their kiss.

She cleared her throat and looked everywhere else but at him. "I seem to have forgotten my manners. Can I get you something to drink?"

"I'm fine." Trey followed her to the hallway and almost bumped into her as she came to an abrupt stop. "The question is are you okay?"

She met his gaze as she toyed with a lock of her hair. "I'm fine. I'm just trying to remember where the kitchen is."

"Ahh, the kitchen," Trey repeated. "My mother considers it the most important room in the house. My father thinks it's the basement."

Her brow furrowed. "Why the basement?"

"It's the only room in the house she let him decorate. My dad went all out with the home theater, wine cellar, bar and a billiards table."

"Speaking about your mother. You'd better go. You don't want to keep her waiting."

"I forgot to take a look at Lucky," Trey said.

"Lucky?" she repeated.

"The iguana."

She blinked and then laughed. "Uncle Camden named him Lucky?"

"It is a she and your uncle rescued Lucky from his backyard."

"I'm not an expert in reptiles, but an iguana of her size is not native to the American Southeast."

"You're right. The best we could come up with is that one of his neighbors decided to give her up because she'd grown too large to keep in fish tank. It's an appropriate name." He pointed to Lucky who seemingly slept under one of the sunlamps. "It's a rags to riches story. How many iguanas do you know outside of the zoo that get their own custom built habitat, room service and medical treatment?"

Sasha laughed. "So he took in a homeless lizard. That sounds just like something that Uncle Camden would do. Any other adventures you want to tell me about?"

"Ask me that question one night after drinks. You wouldn't believe me if I told you when you were sober."

"I will save that for another time." Sasha reached up and ran her fingers through her hair. Mrs. Blackfox's stylist, Fredrick, had done an excellent job. "Please tell your mother 'thank you' for me."

"You could join us for dinner and deliver the message in person."

"Thank you for the invitation." Sasha faked a wide yawn. "But I'm going to turn in. I guess I haven't completely adjusted to the time change."

From the skeptical look on his face, she could tell that Trey wasn't buying her act. But she hoped that he'd be a gentleman and let it pass. She'd had a hard time dodging his mother's questions and an even harder time not giving away the fact that even after just having met her son, she liked Trey more then she cared to admit.

"She'll be disappointed," he pointed out.

That was something Sasha didn't doubt for a moment. "Good night, Trey."

"I'll see you tomorrow when you come to pick up Darwin. Then I'll let you in on a little proposition."

"That sounds ominous."

He stepped closer and leaned down. Sasha's entire body stilled as every nerve seemed to focus on Trey. His cheek brushed against hers and the feel of his lips against her skin sent a shiver down to the tips of her newly French manicured toenails.

"Don't forget to lock the door behind me."

"Yes, sir."

He turned and left her standing there in the foyer. When the door clicked shut behind him, Sasha stared at the wood paneling as it settled on her that she was alone in the huge mansion. She jumped out of her skin when something brushed up against her leg. Zaza began to rub her head against Sasha's pants. "Well, it's just us girls." She bent down and rubbed her head. "How about we head back to the kitchen and fix up some dinner?"

Twenty minutes later Trey leaned against the door-frame and pressed a doorbell to the company-owned condominium in the heart of Buckhead. When the door swung open, he sauntered inside and enveloped his mother in a big hug. "Ready to go out?" Trey asked.

After spending thousands on hotel accommodations

when in town for business, his brother Marius had purchased the three-bedroom luxury home even before the contractor had broken ground. Without waiting for an answer, he slipped by her and stood in the middle of the open foyer.

"I was on the verge of calling you." She tapped her foot.

He turned around from gazing out the large curtainless windows. "Sorry, it took a little longer than I expected to find Sasha's place."

At the mention of Sasha's name, Trey wanted to hit himself as he caught a flash of excitement cross his mother's face. "You took so long I ordered in Chinese. Before you ask, I ordered a large portion of the sweet and sour chicken, an egg roll, hot and sour soup and a few extra fortune cookies."

He walked over and enveloped her in a bear hug. "You're the greatest."

"Yes. I love you, too. Now, wash your hands. The table is set."

After getting out of the bathroom, Trey took a seat at the oval dining room table. He looked over and noted that there were place settings for three people. He hadn't been able to break his chopsticks before she brought up the topic that he'd hoped to avoid.

"I had thought you would invite Sasha to dine with us."

"She turned me down."

"Really?"

"Yep."

"Did you try to change her mind?"

Trey looked away from his mother's discerning gaze and did an elaborate job of spreading his napkin on his lap.

"Thought so. Well, tell me about Sasha."

"You must be off your game today, Mom. Back in the day, all I had to do was miss picking up my phone on the first ring and you'd have the girl's name, age and social security number. You mean that after spending an entire afternoon with Sasha you didn't get her biography and references?"

His mother narrowed her eyes and pointed her chopsticks in his direction. "Cute, son. She's a very intelligent and refreshing young woman. But I didn't ask many questions because I didn't want to scare her off with the nosey-mother routine."

"What about me?" His voice rose. "You ask me questions all the time."

"You don't count. You're my son. It's expected that I pry into your personal life."

"She's new in town and she's going to be a very import art client and benefactor of the clinic."

"And?" his mother asked expectantly.

He popped a pineapple into his mouth. Before leaving the clinic to take Sasha home, he'd gotten a call from the Atlanta zoo inviting him to sit in on a meeting next week. Apparently, the board of directors had given the green light to start a new outdoor exhibit. The planned occupants would be a set of ten golden lion tamarins, which were native to Brazil and would greatly enhance the zoo's primate exhibit. There would need to be a lot of work done to build a suitable habitat and he couldn't think of anyone more qualified than Sasha to assist with the project. "I'm hoping that she'll help at the zoo."

"Trey, stop beating around the bush. Are you going to sleep with the woman, then dump her when you get bored?"

He was so caught off guard by his mother's question that he dropped a piece of chicken. Trey felt his heart rate accelerate, and he forced his eyes not to drop. What had Sasha told his mother about the attorney's office?

"Don't look so shocked. I've heard about your exploits. Your reputation of a lady's man. Brandon brags that you're following in his footsteps."

"It's not like that."

"It better not be. One die-hard bachelor in this family is more than enough. I cannot believe that your grandfather hasn't done something about him."

Trey's brow knitted. The youngest of his father's siblings, Brandon Blackfox had taken his inheritance and started a law firm. Brandon was one of the best corporate attorneys in Georgia, and whenever Trey needed legal advice he called his uncle. Trey had grown up seeing his uncle as a second father.

Brandon's fiancée had died in a car accident and

he'd vowed never to marry. That didn't keep the women from trying to get him down the aisle and his uncle from making appearances at V.I.P social events with a beautiful escort on his arm. Yet, it was a surprise to hear how much his uncle's lack of a wife worried his mother. "I've got too much work to be out in the nightclubs. I barely date."

"That's not what Dr. Robinson told me today."

Trey took a long drink of tea and wished he hadn't left his cell phone in the car. He could have called to check in and concocted an emergency at the clinic to get away. His mother's determined look let him know that he wouldn't be leaving the dining room table without bearing his soul or at least opening up his black book and giving his mother a high-level overview of his personal life. The thing was that he couldn't fault her for her actions. How could he? Her only concern was his happiness. And that alone had him leaning back in his seat, embarrassed at what he imagined his partner had described. "Don't believe everything you hear."

"So you're not a jet-setting playboy wooing women in four states?"

"Four?" He shook his head. "No. Two, maximum."

"Trey," his mother said, and sighed in disappointment.

She stood up and came over to his side of the table. Her hands rested on his shoulders and Trey wanted to scrunch down. He felt as if he was about three years old and he'd just been caught with his hand in the toilet bowl.

"You need to settle down, son."

"I bought a loft," he responded.

"You should have bought a house," she scolded softly. "I had a nice one picked out for you."

"I'm not ready for that."

"Will you ever be? It's time that you grow up and start a family."

"I'm the youngest, remember? Marius and Caleb need to go first."

"Don't you think I've talked to them about this before? Your father and I won't always be around."

"Mom."

"No, you need to listen. I worry about all of you all the time. I just want you to be happy."

"I am. I've got a thriving practice and the challenge of working on the special projects at the zoo."

"But want about your personal life? What about all the wonderful things that you can give to a child? You will make a great father, baby. And your father and I don't want you to miss out on that joy."

He sighed in surrender. He couldn't argue with his mother. None of them could. The five foot six inches, sixty-four-year-old woman commanded four grown men with the inflection of her voice and the look in her eyes.

"I hear you and I'll think about it," he said sheepishly.

"Good." She walked over and returned to her seat on the opposite side of the dining room table. "Do you need any help? I have quite a few friends on the national board."

"No need. I've already got someone in mind."

"Really? What's her name?"

Trey froze and then blurted out the name of the first woman who came to mind. "It's Sasha."

His mother smiled and his heart joined the sweet-and-sour chicken churning in his stomach.

"Wonderful. You know that your father and I are going to Bermuda next month."

"Uh-huh. Grandmother and Grandfather going, too?"

"Yes. We're going to take the yacht right after Grandfather's birthday. I'm planning a get-together and you should bring Sasha."

"She travels a lot. Might not be in country," he hastily replied.

"Either way, promise me that you'll at least invite her? She can be my guest. Sasha is beautiful enough to pull Marius away from work for a few hours."

Oh, hello, no. Trey took a gulp of his drink. The last thing he wanted was to introduce Sasha Clayton to his oldest brother. Women loved Trey, but they lusted after Marius. His parents had hired only male babysitters because the girls had always wanted to flirt with him.

"I'll ask her about her schedule," was the best

response he could come up with on the spur of the moment.

Rose put down her chopsticks and politely patted her lips with the napkin. "You can do better than that."

"I'll invite her to the party," he said.

His mother beamed at him while he added a mental caveat—*after he'd had Sasha between his sheets.*

Chapter 7

Keep your head on straight and you can accomplish anything. Sasha had heard her mother repeat the adage numerous times, and for the most part she'd believed it...until she had walked into her uncle's study and sat behind the large desk staring at stacks of paperwork for two hours.

Falling back into the chair, she dropped the pen in her hand and massaged her aching wrist.

"I thought you could use some tea."

She looked up to see Jackson. "Thank you."

He placed the silver tray on the table and turned to leave.

"Jackson, please. Won't you join me?"

He blinked in surprise and nodded. "I'll go get a cup."

Sasha sighed with relief. She was used to being alone. She'd enjoyed it, but the silence of this house overwhelmed her. Not to mention the lack of things to do. She'd awoken that morning prepared to feed her new pets, only to find that Jackson had not only taken care of the animals, but had also prepared breakfast for her.

By the time he'd returned, Sasha had poured herself a cup and moved to take a seat at a small table next to the window. She smiled at the butler when he re-entered the room, and took the seat opposite her.

"Is Jackson your first or last name?" she asked.

"I was born Jackson Winton II."

"Are you from North England, as well?"

"No, I was born in Liverpool."

"Is that where you met Uncle Camden?"

"No, we met in a holding cell at a London jail," he said with a serious expression. "Camden and a group of environmental protesters had been picked up for handcuffing themselves to a fence outside of Parliament."

Sasha sat forward, her cup of tea forgotten. "Uncle Camden was arrested?"

One corner of Jackson's mouth turned up. "Your godfather was quite the radical in his youth."

"And you were arrested, as well?"

"No, my dear." He shook his head and a chuckle

escaped his lips. "I wasn't the kind of man to have been that idealistic and foolish. I was in jail on charges of theft."

"You've got to be kidding?"

He sat back. "Afraid not. My mother died at child-birth and the old man dropped me off at an orphanage when I was ten years old. When I was eighteen, I'd hitchhiked to London with only a few pounds in my pocket. I fell in with a group of kids and learned how to make easy money lifting merchandise from stores and partaking in a bit of illegal gambling."

"Now, that's a surprise. You don't…"

He finished her sentence. "Seem like the law breaking type?"

Sasha bit her bottom lip to keep from smiling. "I was going to say that you don't fit the mold of any gambler that I've ever met."

"Have you ever visited Las Vegas?"

She shook her head. "I spent a few weeks at the Grand Canyon during a field study."

"Well, gamblers cross all walks of life."

Still curious, she asked, "So Jackson, how did you end up working for Uncle Camden?"

"Your uncle was a smart man, particularly because he knew his own weaknesses and strengths. Twenty-four hours in a smelly concrete room and being the only occupants not thoroughly soused, we did quite a bit of talking. Camden had a passion for saving the environ-ment and he realized early on that he could use his trust fund to fuel his ambitions. He never really explained why he chose to engage a barrister to take on my case, why he arranged for my matriculation into university or why he hired me to manage his affairs while he worked abroad, but he believed in me and I did my best by him."

She sipped her tea as the look of affection on Jackson's face conjured up a question that she'd left unvoiced for years. From behind her closed eyelids she reflected on every meeting, every moment she'd spent with her godfather. Piecing together the memories wove an unfinished tapestry. She could never figure out why her uncle spent his life as a bachelor. She'd met two of his female companions and they had both been intelligent, rich and attractive. She'd never doubted her godfather's sexual orientation or that he'd be a great father. But…

"Jackson, can I ask you a personal question?"

He nodded. "Of course. Keep in mind that I may choose not to answer."

Sasha nibbled on the bottom lip. "Were you and my godfather…" She paused trying to thing of an appropriate word.

"Lovers?"

Sasha felt heat rise from the nape of her neck to the top of her head. All she could do was nod.

"I wondered when you would ask that question."

She sputtered. "I just keep trying to find a reason for why he never married."

"Rest assured your godfather fancied the women and they loved him. He never talked about it, but I always had the feeling that he'd been in love once and it had ended badly."

"I've had my fair share of heartbreak, but I haven't given up hope and I'm sure Uncle Camden would feel the same. He just had so much to give."

"And he did give to charity, animal rights, field research, his organizations, the community and his pets. Your godfather was a simple man in a complex world. And there's one thing that we both know is that when he's made a decision, he goes about his business with an unwavering determination. It wouldn't be a surprise to know that once he gave his heart, he'd never give it to another."

Suddenly things became clear in her mind. "He was like a father to you," she said softly.

Jackson looked down at his cup. "More than the man who left me at the orphanage."

His statement summed up why he'd stayed to manage the estate and why he continued to take care of Sasha. Her godfather had left Jackson two million dollars in his will. He was free to enjoy a life of leisure, but he'd stayed to look after her. Of course, it was more than loyalty that tied Jackson to her uncle—it was love.

Sasha reached out a hand and placed it on his arm to get his attention. "Thank you."

His hand reached out and grasped hers. "He may have treated me like a son, but he loved you like a daughter, Sasha."

She swallowed past the lump in her throat. "I know. The hard part is that I don't understand why he left me all that money."

"Because you want to save the world." He grinned.

She looked over at the antique wall clock. "I guess I should start by picking Darwin up from the vet."

"I can do that for you."

"No," she said quickly. "I'd like to speak with Dr. Blackfox."

"I think that would be a good idea."

"Could I borrow your car?"

"There is no need to borrow. The cars are yours to do with as you wish. Not to mention, I can drive you, Sasha."

"I know. It's just that I feel funny about being driven when I can drive. Plus, I'm sure you have better things to do than drive me from point A to B."

"All right. This way."

They walked down the hallway, past the entertainment room, the kitchen and the laundry. Finally, Jackson opened a door and flipped a light switch to the garage. Sasha blinked rapidly as her eyes adjusted to the florescent lights. "Goodness," she said, stepping away from him.

"Which would you like? They are all in excellent condition and full of gas."

Sasha's gaze started at the left. Mercedes, BMW, convertible Masarati, Bentley. She'd been around rich people. For a period of time she'd lived in the palace

of a Middle Eastern prince while training his pet
cheetahs. But this was different because she'd never
been offered the keys. She thought back to the first car
she'd ever driven. The family had been on an expedition in the middle of Bolivia at the time of her fifteenth
birthday.

Her father had put her behind the wheel of a straight
shift, diesel truck that couldn't have been less than
two decades old. It backfired every ten miles and the
shocks were nonexistent but it was the best vehicle
she'd ever known. Because of her travels, she never
needed a car outside of work and now she apparently
owned four.

Sasha nibbled on the inside of her lip before turning
back to Jackson. His eyes held a devilish crinkle of
amusement as if he could sense her discomfort. "How
about the least expensive one."

Trey looked down at the sheets of expenditures and
revenues and sighed heavily. Even having hired one of
the best accounting firms in Atlanta, nothing seemed
to keep him from having to do paperwork. Every other
month it was his duty to review the clinic's finances and
he hated it. Almost as much as he disliked looking at
his personal finances. Yet, his uncle and father's
warnings always seemed to come to the forefront.
Never take the Blackfox name for granted, thank God
for every breath you take, never get complacent and
always keep an eye on your money. He looked around

the office that he'd help design in the building he'd paid to build, and that sense of rightness returned.

Samuel Graham Veterinary Clinic was one of a handful of not-for-profit operations in the southeast devoted to pet care. He'd started the clinic in the memory of his late grandfather on his mother's side. Trey had spared no expense in creating a pet-friendly environment with state-of-the-art technology. He'd had to use a combination of charm and bribery to start the practice three years after his veterinary internship. The people who worked at the clinic were more than adequately compensated for their skills and willingness to sometimes work long hours.

Each patient was charged a fee based on income and in emergencies no pet was turned away. The clientele covered the spectrum of Georgia's population—from drug dealers and the income challenged of Atlanta's inner city, to corporate executives, sports figures and politicians. He'd treated scores of geriatric dogs and cats with everything from renal disease to cancer. On any given day, he and the other four vets treated rabbits, iguanas, birds and chinchillas. Not to mention the high-strung owners of pedigree champions or spoiled-rotten mongrels.

Deep in thought, Trey hadn't heard the footsteps of someone entering his office.

"Dude, it's fate."

"What?"

"She studies animals. I help them. She just moved

to Atlanta. I did, too. She's into documentaries and I'm a history minor—we're perfect for one another."

If he hadn't looked up at his assistant, Trey would have sworn the dreadlocked intern was a blonde surfer fresh from the California coast. He shook his head. Jo had only been with them for three months but in that short time he'd proved himself to be a valuable member of their staff. Jo fell hard and fast for a girl. Trey, on the other hand, didn't fall at all. He reached out and picked up another bound report. "So who's the new crush?" he asked off-handedly.

"Sasha Clayton."

Now, that got his attention. Technically the lady wasn't his type. She had commitment written all over her. She didn't want or need his money, high maintenance wasn't in her vocabulary, and he could see himself getting along with her too well. They had too much in common. Regardless, the memory of her tear-stained face hadn't been too far from his thoughts in the last twenty-four hours. Trey stood up and began to straighten out his desk. "Don't go there, my man."

"Serious, Trey. She's got a rich uncle. No, wait. She *had* a rich uncle. I've got a rich boss and thirty thousand in student loans."

"She's older than you."

"Age is just a number on a driver's license. Besides I've never been a boy toy before."

"Jo, we're not having this conversation. This clinic is not a bar and Sasha Clayton is not only a client, she's off limits—" he paused "—to you."

Jo raised and lowered his chin as a super-size smile lit his face. "Oh, now I get it. Dude, you can't take the competition."

"No, I can't take the noise and I'm fresh out of tissues for your future broken heart."

"Whatever, you'll see that she likes me."

"I'll bet that she like animals, kids and old people, too."

"You're cold, Trey." Jo pretended to shiver. "Icy. You might want to try some bedside manners. Take a people skills class. You know, relate to us regular people."

"I'll put that on my schedule. Now could you bring Darwin into room four, please?"

"Oh my God!" Jo exclaimed, and placed his hands over his heart in feigned shock. "The man said 'please.' It's a miracle."

Trey picked up his stethoscope and hung it around his neck, all the while laughing. This was what got him up in the morning and kept him coming back although he had enough money to pursue any situation he wanted. The people and the animals. The fact that he was not only needed but also wanted. He grinned—it didn't help that being nice to animals was always a help with the ladies.

Trey Blackfox had the most unbelievable complexion, Sasha observed as he entered the room with Darwin in his arms. The deep brown shade was so smooth she couldn't believe that he'd ever had a pimple. Just looking at him made her want to touch. Good looking and warm clear eyes with chestnut colored irises.

Earlier, Sasha hadn't even looked at the chair after the assistant had led her into the examination room. All she wanted to do was pace. And because there wasn't enough space in the ten-by-ten space, she began to examine the objects on the countertops and the numerous pictures of various animal, bird and reptile life.

Trey paused for a moment and just seemed to stare at her intently before placing sitting Darwin on the examination table. More nervous than she should have been, Sasha stepped closer and smiled. "You look surprised to see me."

"You're early," he replied with a half grin she felt all the way down to her toes.

She shook her head and shyly glanced away. Instinct made her want to stare at him and purr like a cat watching a canary. Good old common sense, however, grabbed her by the back of the neck and made her look down and focus on the tile flooring and how nice it looked in contrast to her shoes. She drew in a deep breath before responding. "I was worried about Darwin."

"That's the first step in becoming a responsible pet owner. Before you know it you'll be planning your life around your pet."

"Seems that way. Looks like I'll be here for a while,"

she answered simply. As soon as the words left her mouth, Sasha's stomach flipped. Somehow she'd known since the moment the plane had circled the campsite in Malaysia, her life would never be the same.

"Well, I think Darwin and I are in agreement."

"On what?"

"We're both glad that you're going to be sticking around."

She smiled and placed her hand under Darwin's chin and scratched. "Will he going to be alright?"

"With a little TLC and a prescription diet to increase his appetite, he'll be barking up a storm and digging up holes in the backyard in no time."

"Thank you," Sasha rushed and in her excitement stepped forward and hugged Trey. She buried her face in his shoulder and just breathed for a moment as the rush of relief almost made her weak in the knees.

Speechless for a moment, Trey's arms hung on the side and after his brain kicked in, he lifted his arms and only gave her a quick squeeze while a part of him wanted to toss caution out the door and kiss Sasha like he had last night. "Just doing my job," he partially mumbled into the top of her head.

When she drew back, he cleared his throat and stuck his hands in his pants pockets. "Now that we've gotten one thing pretty much squared away, when do you think you'll be able to handle the heavy stuff?"

"What heavy stuff?"

"Finding someone to take over for your godfather's foundation?"

"That. To be honest, I don't know as to where to start. The attorneys sent over an encyclopedia-size stack of resumes."

"You only have to ask and I'll be there to help."

"Thank you. I have a feeling that I'll be needing help soon."

"Then we'll have an even trade because I need yours, as well."

Her brow furrowed. "You need my help?"

He nodded. "Now that I know you'll be sticking around, I have a project that's perfect for you."

"Trey, really, I'm not sure how long I'll be staying. I've never not been traveling."

"Wait before you turn me down. At least see what it is I'm asking for."

"Why don't you just tell me?"

He grinned. "Have you ever heard of a car salesman who could sell a car sight unseen?"

"Well…" Sasha smiled.

"Exactly. It's not really possible if there's no trust and you can't see exactly what you'll be getting. So we'll have dinner Thursday night and work on establishing trust. Friday, how about you meet me at Atlanta zoo about eleven a.m? We can have lunch afterwards and come up with a plan to tackle those resumes."

"I'm not making any promises."

"And I'm not asking you to make any. Just think about it and drop by. If you don't, then give me a call." Trey pulled a business card from his pocket. "My cell phone number is in the bottom right corner. You can call anytime."

When Trey got back to his office later that afternoon after a consult at the zoo, the sun was blazing through the windows and the smell of lemon deodorizer permeated the air. Harriet, the office manager, smiled after dropping a bundle of mail in his inbox, and Johann Pachelbel's Canon in D Major played over the intercom system. *So much to do and so little time,* Trey thought. He dropped his notebook on the wooden desktop, pulled out his leather chair, logged on to his computer, and prepared to update the health records of his patients. The first one up for entry would be to order a second round of tests on Ruffle, a seizuring Akita mix.

His phone buzzed before the receptionist's voice came over the intercom. "Dr. Blackfox, I have Jared Gresham on line one."

Trey grinned. "Thank you." He hit the button and leaned back in his chair. "Speak on it, brother."

"Man, Trey, you are a genius."

His brows shot upwards as he searched his memory for the reason behind his best friend's declaration. It took him a few seconds to recall Big Boy, the Labrador retriever with an almost fatal penchant for chocolate. "I take it he's recovered?"

"He's back at home stirring up trouble," Jared said.

"That's good," Trey replied.

"That's not all," Jared continued. "I'm looking down at two sets of courtside season tickets for all of this season's Hawks home games."

"Congratulations," Trey replied.

"No, my brother. Congratulations to you. The second set is yours. Dang, man, I just tell you about tickets most people would kill for and you're not even excited."

"It's just I've got other things on my mind at the moment."

"Your family okay?"

"Yeah, everybody's fine. My mother's busy planning my grandfather's birthday."

"Okay, if the family's well and I know that you're not having work or money problems, then what's her name?"

"Who?"

"The female that's keeping you from doing a happy dance."

"You're nuts," Trey said. "I'm just busy with work."

"Cool, you don't want to talk about her yet. I understand. I was like that in the beginning, too. Now on to the other two things I called to talk to you about."

"There's more?"

"Yep. Can I put you down for Steve's bachelor party?"

"Wouldn't miss it for the world," Trey responded wryly. Damn. The last thing he wanted to do was sit through hours of reminiscing about the way things were in college, how many women he'd be giving up, the days of jetting to the West Coast for a party or the fact that he would be giving up all of his closet space and selling his two-seater Mercedes convertible.

"Good. You might want to take notes at the party because you're on the hook for mine."

"Is it that serious between you and Rochelle?"

"Don't tell anybody, but I stopped by a jewelry shop on the way home the other day. Man, I almost had an asthma attack at the prices. I felt like I was buying a piece of Africa when I looked at some of those solitaires."

"That's the price you pay for eternal happiness," Trey sarcastically replied.

"Anyway, you got anything going on tomorrow night because the Hawks are playing at home."

"Who are they playing?"

"Seattle."

"What are the odds on Atlanta winning?" Trey asked.

"Pretty good. Devon's betting they'll be up by twenty points before the second quarter."

He rubbed a hand across his head and sighed. It was going to be a good game. It had to be. Seattle had a superstar defense and for the first time in a decade, Atlanta had some key players, but Trey couldn't go because he'd already made dinner reservations. Not that he wasn't tempted, but the thought of sitting across from Sasha and watching her lips as she bit into a juicy steak did more for him then watching his home team.

"I can't go."

"What—better offer?"

"Something like that. It's dinner."

"Gotta be a women. You can't fool me, Trey. I've known you for too long. What is she? A model, attorney, real estate agent? Don't tell me she's a singer because that's just a cover for her real job as a stripper."

"It's a business dinner."

"Yeah, right," Jared sarcastically replied.

Jo came through the door and sat on the corner of Trey's desk. "What'd she say?"

"What did who say?"

"Sasha Clayton." Jo's head bobbed up and down. "I was cleaning out the kennel so I missed her when she picked up Darwin. I know she said something about me."

"No," Trey replied curtly.

"Come on, Trey. Don't hate on a player. It's all over the office that the two of you were in the examination room too long just to be discussing the dog's health."

"Who's Sasha?" Jared yelled out over the speaker-phone.

Trey refocused his attention on the phone. "A client."

"What's she say about me?" Jo asked again.

"I'm serious. She didn't say anything about you."

Jo narrowed his eyes at Trey. "Is that a lipstick stain I see on your coat?"

He followed the direction of the intern's stare and sure enough, the twin half circles of bronze marked his shoulder. "Looks like it."

"What happened?"

"We talked," Trey said, losing patience. "She's a liberal, soft-hearted, wildlife researcher, who happens to have inherited money, pets and a responsibility to help run our foundation. I also happen to think that she'd be perfect to help design a new primate habitat at the zoo."

"That's all well and good, but how did the lipstick get on your collar? She tripped?"

Trey reached over and pulled the collar of his white coat down. Sure enough, he saw to half-moon crescents of Sasha's shade of burnt auburn lipstick. "She hugged me."

"She hugged you?" Jo exclaimed.

His intern made it sound like he'd had sex with the woman in the examination room table. Trey's eyes slid away. Damn sure he'd thought about it often enough.

"She was relieved to hear that Darwin was going to be fine," Trey explained.

Jo blew air out of his nose and leaned back against the wall. "Yeah, right."

"And I asked her out to dinner. Strictly to talk about a zoo project and—" finally, Trey put his hands behind his head, gave up the facade of disinterest and let his real feelings come out "—and to see if the sparks can catch fire."

"I knew there had to be a woman involved," Jared

chimed in. "Trey, you've got one shot to score. Don't slip up or you'll be trapped in the friendship zone."

"Yeah, I know. I'm going all out. The plan is to borrow Regan's corvette and take her out to dinner. Leather seats, sports car, a nice dinner and a few glasses of wine."

"Playa, playa. I'll just have to give the Hawks tickets to someone else," Jared said.

"Did I hear something about giving away Hawks tickets?"

Trey and Jo both turned to Emilio, who stared back, muscular, tanned and anxious in the florescent light from the hallway. "The girl I'm dating is a big Hawks fan."

Jared's sigh came through clearly over the speaker-phone. "I'll have someone deliver your half of the tickets this afternoon."

"All right"

Trey looked at Emilio. "I'll drop the tickets off at your office later."

Emilio's eyes bugged out. "Serious?" He took another step into Trey's office. He looked around—it was now a full house. All he needed now was the rest of the staff to come in to have an impromptu meeting on his personal life.

"Courtside seats. I'm sure your date will be over-joyed."

"Courtside? Ahh, man." Jo hit himself on the head. Trey saw disappointment on his face.

"What about me?" Jo asked after taking a seat in the leather office chair.

"Emilio asked first."

"I was going to ask," Jo shot back.

"Too late for this game." Trey paused and looked back and forth between the veterinarian and the intern. "Unless you two want to go together?"

"Nah."

Trey decided that he would give Jo the tickets to the next game, but he'd wait until there wasn't such a large audience. He was known for his generosity, only because he had so much to give. His financial situation wasn't a secret and he enjoyed giving nice gifts to his staff.

"Next game, Jo."

His normal beach-boy smile returned. "How about tickets to the Lakers and Hawks?"

"What?" Trey howled. Without a doubt, the game would be one of the best of the season. Anytime there was an East coast versus West coast match, the atmosphere intensified the rivalry on the court and in the stands.

"You took my future wife." Jo tried to look injured, but to Trey he just looked constipated. "The least you can do is hand over a few tickets."

"All right. But this stays between us."

"Cool."

"Great, now we're all going to be here until midnight if we don't get back to work," Trey said. "Start with getting the urinary samples from the Manx that came into emergency last night."

Jo stood up quickly and backed away from Trey's desk. "You know I don't like working with cats, especially big cats. Not to mention I'm more of a canine man. I never have problems with them because they recognize that I'm the boss."

Trey shook his head and began to gather together some of the paperwork on his desk. "Said by a man who ran from a dog with a broken leg."

"The dog in question was a hundred-pound German shepherd with a cast on his leg."

Trey laughed just remembering the episode, and then turned back to his computer. "I'll be waiting for those results."

Chapter 8

It took fifteen minutes of rambling through the bedroom dressers, her suitcases and the closet before Sasha gave up and went in search of Jackson. With Darwin trotting beside her, she knocked on the door to his quarters and, receiving no answer, continued farther into the back of the house. From there she followed the tapping sound into a small workroom. Jackson sat bent over a wooden table with a small hammer.

She stood in the doorway and stared in awe. Model boats with double masts, yachts with double decks, rafts and canoes sat on shelves, which lined the workroom walls. When Sasha realized that the hammering had stopped, Darwin had already crossed the room and sat next to Jackson.

He turned on the stool so that he faced her, hands holding a small piece of wood that she guessed was a boat's rudder. "Good morning, Sasha."

"Jackson, this is incredible."

"Thank you. As your godfather would say, 'A gentleman requires something to do with his hands.' Please come in."

She stepped into the room and went over to the nearest wall. Her eyes locked on the sails to a smaller craft that sat at eye level.

"This must have taken you years to complete."

"That one only took a few months. This one will take me about a year, but it'll be worth it considering that this will be my retirement boat."

"You're quitting?" Sasha's heart gave out at the thought as her mind couldn't fathom handling her uncle's estate and living in the huge house alone.

Jackson stood, took off his working smock, and hung it up. Sasha had to hand it to the man. Not a wrinkle in sight. Sasha wasn't proud to admit that she could count on one hand the number of times she'd picked up an iron.

"No, dear girl. I plan on acquiring the actual boat some day in the near future."

"Not too near, okay?"

"Of course. What can I do for you this morning?"

Sasha's body went limp with relief and, feeling something wet on her ankles, she bent down and gave Darwin a pat on his head. It was remarkable what a little TLC and a change of diet could accomplish.

Shaking her head, she returned her attention to Jackson. "I know this is going to sound strange, but my some of my clothes are missing. I've checked my suitcases, the hampers and the laundry room. I just can't find them."

He nodded as though she'd spoken about something as mundane as the weather. For a moment, Sasha wondered if he would have done the same thing if she'd said aliens were landing in the backyard. "I was wondering when you'd notice."

"Well, I'm dangerously low on underwear and I thought I'd do laundry. Has the housekeeper taken them to the drycleaners?"

The butler smiled as he politely gestured for her to precede him into the hallway. "Not exactly. The housekeeper did take your clothing at my request."

Sasha's brow furrowed at the oddness of his response. After aiming a quizzical glance in his direction, she followed Jackson into the study. "Will I be getting them back anytime soon?" she asked jokingly.

"No. I've had the bulk of your clothes donated to a local shelter."

Her mouth fell open. "What? You…what?"

"They were delivered to the women's shelter yesterday afternoon."

"Excuse me."

"It's time that you realized that this isn't temporary, Sasha, dear. You are the heir to Camden's fortune and you will be a representative for his foundation. It's past the time for you to accept your inheritance."

She didn't say anything for several seconds as her mother's voice echoed in her head. *Think before you speak, butterfly.* On one level, she understood what Jackson was doing. She didn't like him for it, but she understood. Still, her parents didn't call her stubborn for nothing. "I want my clothes back," she said at last.

"You can't have them back."

She crossed her arms and glared as he smiled back at her. "You had no right to give them away. They were perfectly decent clothes."

"Only for tramping around in some third world country or digging in the garden." He picked up a letter-size envelope from the desk. "This contains the resumes of highly recommended wardrobe consultants in New York, Atlanta, Paris, Los Angeles and London. As soon as you let me know which of them is agreeable, I will make an arrangement on your behalf. You'll also find a cheque register, ATM and American Express Platinum cards. If you need others, the bankers would be more than happy to oblige."

Sasha shook her head. *Bankers.* Not just one but a whole team had paid her a visit yesterday. She couldn't remember the last time she'd stepped into a bank and done something other than exchange currency. "This is crazy. Women like me just don't wake up one morning and turn into jet-setting money spenders. I was happy without all this, Jackson. I was happy with my beat-up khakis, worn-out jeans, T-shirts and wool sweaters."

He smiled and lightly patted her shoulder. "Then

you, dear girl, will be positively ecstatic with your new clothing, as well."

"Are you not listening to me?"

"I hear you perfectly. My eyesight has weakened with age and I do have a tendency to feel the cold more than I used to in my younger years, but my hearing has not diminished according to my physician."

"You could have just mentioned that I might want to pick up some clothes."

"I have. In fact, not only have I mentioned it to you for the last week, I also took the liberty of placing catalogs on your bedside table."

Her shoulders slumped and she looked down. Arguing with him would only give her a headache. Sasha looked down at her shoes and another thought popped into her head.

"Please tell me that you didn't give away my shoes?"

"No."

Sasha moved and sank into the chair with relief. Her hiking boots were the closest things she could come to a lucky charm. They'd helped her climb trees to escape hyena, run from a swarm of angry bees, swim across swollen African rivers and kept her toes from frostbite on more than one occasion. She could replace the clothing, but her feet, all of her blisters, calluses and achy toes, knew every centimeter of those boots.

"No, I'm afraid those were beyond salvageable. I put them in the trash."

She bolted out of the chair. "When?"

"Yesterday."

"Has the garbage been picked up?"

"Tomorrow."

"Thank you, Lord," she whispered. Without a backward glance, Sasha sprinted out of the study and headed toward the garage.

Twenty minutes later, she returned to the study and held up her prize boots. It had only taken Sasha a minute to open the garbage bin and locate them, but instead of marching back into the house and blowing up at Jackson, she calmly located the bathroom off the kitchen, washed her hands and splashed water on her face.

Jackson gave her a strange look. "You actually removed those out of the trash bin?"

She smiled. "They were right on top."

His gaze zoomed in on the boots she held in her hand. Sasha barely squelched the urge to place them behind her back. "I'm keeping the boots."

"I see."

"And I can pick out my own clothes."

"Of course, you are a woman. Nevertheless, a second opinion never hurts. Especially if one has a dinner invitation from a certain veterinarian."

Trey. She hadn't forgotten about the event and forgotten that she'd told Jackson. Somehow between meetings and feedings, she'd pushed it to the furthest reaches of her mind. "That's tomorrow night. Do I have enough time?"

"I'll schedule an afternoon appointment and have lunch catered."

* * *

The next evening after a couple of wardrobe changes and a half hour of viewing herself in the closet's floor-length mirror, Sasha hung up the cashmere trousers and blouse she'd planned to wear and slipped on a V-neck, knit dress. As bad as she hated to admit it, the luxury of being able to shop without looking at price tags or worrying about going over her budget had felt extremely good. With the attentive presence of the wardrobe consultant Jackson hired, Sasha had ended up with a trunk full of clothing, shoes and accessories. While looking into the mirror, she slid her hand down the side and smiled. "Not too bad, Sasha, girl."

She turned and walked into the bathroom. As she began to pull out makeup brushes, compacts and lipsticks from her newly purchased cosmetics bag, she thought about her upcoming dinner with Trey Blackfox.

There was something about his deep voice and the calm way that he spoke that lingered in her waking thoughts and appealed to her soul. Somehow, Trey had managed to put her at ease every time they met. He was funny, down to earth and passionate about his work. She yearned to know more about him. Until now, she'd only felt that way about her work. The only difference was, she wanted to get close to Trey instead of studying him from afar.

At six o'clock, she got behind the wheel of her godfather's silver BMW sedan and drove toward downtown Atlanta. Luckily, traffic had begun to die down so she made her way to Peachtree Street and pulled the car into the drive. The valet nodded appreciatively at both Sasha and the car. The look from a man barely over the legal drinking age boosted her confidence enough to bring a smile to her heart-shaped lips. Stepping through the doors, Sasha swallowed a bout of nervousness. Steady, she told herself. Just dinner with a new friend, not a date. This will just be a walk in the park. When I see him, she thought, I'll probably wonder why I spent the past two hours getting ready.

As soon as she passed through the entrance, Sasha was brought to a stop. She'd dined in restaurants around the world, but the entrance room's grand rotunda and ascending marble staircase was something out of a classic movie.

"Good evening, Ms. Clayton," an unknown voice said. Sasha shook her head and turned her attention to the suit-clad host.

"How did you know my name?"

He smiled. "Dr. Blackfox gave a very good description of you."

Sasha couldn't help but return his smile. "Did he?"

"In essence," he replied and then winked an eye. "You're much prettier, though. Now if you would allow me to escort you to your date?"

Sasha was glad to have someone to follow as she walked into the main room. The restaurant was elegantly designed with lush fabrics, soft leathers, wooden murals and marble columns. Italian chandeliers hung from the dining room's gilt-accented ceiling. Although she'd been pulled into the atmosphere, Sasha immediately spotted Trey sitting at the bar sipping a drink.

Damn, she silently cursed. Sasha felt a bit awkward as heads turned in her direction until Trey stood and walked her way. The relaxed confidence he seemed to exude was more seductively powerful than any mythical aphrodisiac she'd come across in her travels.

As she walked toward him, Sasha couldn't seem to focus on anything else and although soft music played in the background, all she could hear was the beating of her heart.

He stopped and the appreciative smile on his face caused a swarm of butterflies to erupt in her stomach. Before she could voice an appropriate greeting, he took her hand and brought it to his lips in a playful display of affection and immediately she felt the tug of sexual attraction. It made her toes curl in the tight space of the one-size-too-small shoes on her feet. She took a deep breath and the sensation of his lips touching the back side of her hand made her head spin. Although the gesture was done in jest, it left her feeling like Cinderella.

For a moment, she felt self-conscious; remembering that she hadn't been borne to wealth and privilege and the expensive clothes on her back had only had the price tags removed an hour before. She looked around, noticing that all eyes in the room had been drawn to their little show, and blushed.

"Hello, beautiful." His voice brought a deeper blush to her skin.

"Hello, Trey."

Moment's later they settled across from each other over a balcony table that looked out over main dining area. "What can I get you to drink?" the waiter asked after silently materializing beside their table.

"I'll have a glass of Chardonnay," Sasha said. Trey ordered bourbon for himself.

"Any recommendations?" she asked.

"Anything chicken, beef or pork. You won't find better beef unless you take a ride down to South Georgia and hit a juke joint on a Sunday after church."

Sasha pulled her eyes from the man across the table and focused on the menu. She'd dined in some of the best and worst places in the world. Yet the extensive variation on steak, pork and chicken could have rivaled even the most exclusive New York restaurants. Needless to say, when the waiter arrived to deliver their drinks, she ordered the steak and wasn't surprised when Trey did the same.

"I'd like to propose a toast. To healthy pets and happy owners." Trey lifted his glass.

"I'll toast to that," she replied. Sasha squashed a hysterical giggle, feeling like a high school girl sitting next to her crush on the school bus. She clicked her glass against his, then took a sip. The velvety, almost sweet fruity flavor sent a wave of pleased relaxation through her body.

"Did you find the restaurant okay?"

"Yes. You gave excellent directions. The car has one of those navigation systems, but it gives me a headache when I try to follow the directions on the screen and keep from hitting someone at the same time."

Trey's laugh was lethal. It filled her skin and made things warm and fuzzy. Sasha relaxed into her seat. "I wouldn't have believed that there could be so many ways to name a street Peachtree."

"There are actually over fifty streets, roads, boulevards, highways and avenues with 'Peachtree' in the name in Atlanta."

Her smile matched his. "That would be a fact only a native would know."

He shook his head. "If you stay in the city more than a few days, you'll find out the hard way that there's more than one Peachtree. Stay longer and you'll know the exact number."

"So which are you? A native or a newcomer?"

"A little bit of both. I'm from Rome, Georgia."

"Where's that?"

"Just northwest of the city, right next to the North Georgia Mountains."

"So you're not a city boy?" she surmised.

"Not by a long shot," he grinned. "I grew up in the country until it became the suburbs. I spent half my childhood shoveling horse manure, hauling oats, picking hooves, weaning kittens, deworming dogs and helping anything wounded that happened to come my way. I imagine you had the same experience." His eyes held hers, displaying a warmth that challenged her to respond in kind.

That dimple of his was back in full effect. Without a doubt, the slight hollow would appear in her fantasies for a few nights. What was it about Trey that made her want to throw caution to the winds and revert to the basic animal instincts she'd witnessed in her research? How could someone she hadn't known manage to hold such a physical and mental attraction?

"Close. But unlike you, I spent most of my time just watching. There were a few opportunities to take in wounded birds or other small animals. My parents believe in the separation of humans and animals. My father in particular believes the two should only meet on rare occasions."

Trey sat back and snapped his fingers. "Now that explains it."

"Excuse me?" she asked as she sat forward.

"You've just clued me in as to why a woman with an international reputation as an animal researcher, a master's in biology and zoology can't handle a depressed canine."

"How did you know about my degrees?"

"I make it a point to know as much as I can about someone I'm interested in."

No doubt about it. He was interested. Sasha nervously reached out, picked up her wineglass and took a gulp. The slight sting of the crisp white wine knocked the stars out of her eyes and calmed her stomach. She took her time picking up the napkin and wiping her mouth, so she was able to formulate an adequate reply. "I'm not sure if I should be flattered or annoyed. That was a good line, though."

"It's not a line, Sasha." He looked up at her, his warm puppy eyes very brown, very open. "I might not be Prince Charming, but I'm far from being a player. You can call any of my exes and they'll tell you that I am honest."

"So Ms. Ski Bunny and Ms. New York know about each other?"

"They're sorority sisters."

Sasha sat back in her chair and raised an eyebrow. "I'm impressed."

"You've got a suspicious mind, Sasha Clayton. Ms. New York happens to be my little cousin who just started as a lead dancer position with Alvin Ailey Dance Company. Ms. Ski Bunny is—"

He stopped, and she said, "Another cousin?"

"No, nothing that innocent. Kayla and I met six months ago at a conference in Aspen. Mix cold snow with Jamaican rum and you get two consenting adults seeking companionship for a few days."

"Is that what you're looking for here?"

Trey sat forward, and placed his hands on the table.

"Maybe. I won't deny that I've been physically and mentally attracted to you since the first day we met."

Just then, the meal arrived and Sasha was spared having to respond to his provocative declaration.

The filet mignon, baked potato and steamed asparagus could have come fresh from a magazine ad. Needing time to get her brain back into gear, she took refuge in a bite of the baked potato. The butter, sour cream and chives hit her tongue and made a nice smooth descent to her stomach. Deciding to move on to something more substantial, she picked up her steak knife. She could have almost cut the butter-soft grilled meat with her fork. She took a bite, closed her eyes and began to chew. When she'd swallowed, she looked at Trey. *"Heaven,"* Sasha said.

"That good?" Trey asked.

She met his eyes and her heart flipped. "Delicious."

He smiled and then cut into his steak. "Wait until you get a bite of my grilled pork chops."

"You cook?"

"I marinate, sauté, bake and grill," he corrected. "I don't know a Southern boy yet that didn't spend half his summer outside in the backyard with their dad standing at the barbeque pit. Caleb could have been a gourmet chef if he hadn't gone into medicine."

"Caleb?"

"My older brother."

"Right, I remember that you mentioned that you had a brother."

"Yep, two brothers and a younger sister. What about you?"

"I'm an only child."

"So you were the center of attention and the apple of your father's eye?"

"More like coconut," Sasha smiled. "I was my parents' helper from an early age."

"At least you got your own room."

"Sometimes." She smiled. "Other times, I shared it with a hodgepodge of animals I decided to rescue," Sasha said.

"You, too? My mother grounded me for a month for bringing in a stray raccoon. He got loose in the house. What about you?"

If anyone else had asked Sasha about her childhood, she would have glossed over the comical incidents, travel misadventures, exotic trips and cultural faux pas. The idea didn't occur to her with Trey. Over the course of dinner, he regaled her with stories of his family and drew her out with open-ended questions.

"So it's safe to say that you won't be adopting any chinchillas in the near future?" Sasha asked minutes after putting her fork down next to the remaining crumbs of a decadent slice of triple chocolate cake.

"No more pets for me. I'm a pet-free man and I plan to stay that way for a while."

After the waitstaff cleared the table and discreetly left the check, Trey placed some bills in the letter wallet, then came to his feet and helped Sasha out of her chair.

As he held up her coat, Trey allowed himself a glimpse at her exposed skin. He gulped as he looked at the lovely swells of her breasts. He stood back and helped her with her coat. Her best assets were always hidden by clothing, he thought. But that didn't bother him at all—in fact, he got more of a rush imagining what was underneath.

"Thank you for dinner." Sasha's softly spoken words sounded musical to his ears.

"It doesn't have to end, you know."

"We have to go home eventually."

"Yes, and we can go to my place first. I've got the cappuccino maker set to brew—" he glanced down at his watch "—in ten minutes. So how about you follow me back to my place?" He phrased it casually, but it was still an open invitation to a midnight seduction.

Sasha slowly shook her head from side to side. "I don't think that would be a good idea. Remember we're going to keep our relationship strictly professional."

"Nope, I don't remember that one." Trey grinned and handed the valet both of their parking receipts. "Besides, I think that we've already crossed that line."

"When?"

"When you went from my daytime fantasies to my midnight dreams and started keeping me up all night and taking cold showers in the morning."

"That would be another great reason for why you should go to your place and me to mine."

"Come on, aren't you the slightest bit curious about

where I live? Don't you want a peek into the vet's natural habitat?"

Sasha narrowed her eyes on his grinning face. Darn. She did. Just like the wildlife she researched, she wanted to know if he had a house acres from the nearest neighbor, if he had furniture leftover from his college days, if his refrigerator held groceries or take-out boxes. She wondered if his sock drawer was organized by color or if his dirty clothes covered the floor. Not to mention, she wondered if the bathtub would gleam and sparkle or be covered with layers of soap scum. Before she could answer, a man in a suit and tie came to a halt in front of them.

"Excuse me, Mr. Blackfox?"

"Yes."

"My name is Thomas Rayners and I'm the restaurant manager. Could I speak with you for a moment?"

Puzzled, Trey allowed the man to usher them to a more private section of the lobby.

The manager cleared his throat before speaking, "I'm sorry to tell you that we've had a little incident with your vehicle."

Trey felt a sinking feeling in the pit of his stomach. "Don't tell me you put a dent in the car. It's my sister's car and she'll kill me if it's not back in the garage by next weekend. Mr. Rayners, the Corvette is worth more than you, me and Bill Gates."

"It's not that simple and if there had been such an issue, we would have gladly taken care of getting the car repaired. In this case, I'm afraid your car is missing."

Stunned, Trey looked around at the empty circular drive, then back at the manager. "I'm sorry. I thought you just said my car is missing."

"Yes. That's what I said. One of our valets is missing, as well."

For the third time in his life, Trey Blackfox was dumbstruck. This wasn't the first time he'd had a car stolen. He braced for the panic that came from locating the space where he'd parked his car only to find nothing but a patch of broken glass or some tire marks. But he didn't get that sinking feeling. No, his gut was doing a 360 degree turn, and then a nose dive. The Corvette was his baby sister's pride and joy. He'd borrowed it on the promise that he'd not only bring it back with a full tank of gas, but also a fresh coat of wax and interior detailing.

Sasha stepped in. "Have you called the police?"

"We were hoping to not have that happen. Our restaurant has a reputation to uphold. If it gets out that we've got car thieves, I don't know how we'll recover."

"I don't care about your reputation. I need that car and I need it now."

"I'll have a driver take you anywhere you need to go. I'll write you a check for five thousand dollars that you can keep. All I need is for you to give me forty-eight hours to locate the car before you can go to the police."

"Keep the money." Trey pulled his cell phone from his pocket and flipped it open. "I'm calling the police now."

"Look, Mr. Blackfox, if you call the police I can't help you. I have a private detective on retainer who can go places that the police won't and he can go to the boy's friends and family. At Fulton County police department your information will go on to the bottom of a long list. I, on the other hand, won't rest until your car is returned to you."

"That's as close to blackmail as I've ever heard," Sasha interjected.

"Take it or leave it. The chance to get your car back, five thousand dollars and complimentary meals—or spend the next three hours filling out paperwork at the Fulton county police department?"

Trey gave the man a hard stare and returned his cell phone to his pocket. Just because he didn't have much of a choice didn't mean he had to like it. "What do I have to do?"

"Just take a seat in the restaurant. Frank is on his way here and he should arrive in less than ten minutes. Please order a bottle of wine for yourself and your lovely companion. The wine cellar is open to both of you. Name a vintage and it's yours."

The manager's private detective, Frank Turner, didn't live up to his name, Trey thought a half hour later. And for once he was glad of it. Frank had a bald head, scarred knuckles and a broken nose. He was over six feet and built like a tank. Trey wouldn't hesitate to put his money on the P.I. in a fight. Frank skipped all the formalities and started asking questions the second he sat down at their table. "Can you give me the year, make, model and color of the vehicle?"

"It's a 2001 pewter Chevy Corvette."

"Anything distinguishing?

"It's barely street legal, has alloy wheels and it's been modified for racing."

Frank's pen paused for a second, then he looked up. "When was the last time you saw the car?"

"Couple of hours ago when I gave the keys to the valet."

"Did he park it out front?"

"No, I saw him drive it around the back."

Frank removed his sunglasses. "You didn't suspect anything? Did the boy seem nervous?"

"No. He took the keys, gave me the check, and got into the car. The kid didn't gun the engine or anything."

"Do you have a tracking device installed on the vehicle?"

"It's not my car—it's my sister's."

"Did your sister install a tracking device on the car?"

Trey shook his head. "I don't know."

"Can you contact your sister?"

"Can I sign my own death warrant?" he parried. "What are my chances of getting that car back before, let's say, two o'clock next Sunday?"

"An associate will get the VIN number from the registration and check for a tracking ID number. In the meantime, I'll run down anyone who's been in contact with the boy. If I can get him in less than twenty-four hours, then you've got a good chance that you'll get it back intact with a few extra miles on the odometer."

"And if not?"

"Then the car is probably either out of state or in pieces."

Speechless, Trey could barely nod his head. It took him a moment, but he managed to hoarsely respond, "Save a life, man. Find that car."

"I'll do my best," Frank said, giving Trey a confident look. After he took down Trey's phone numbers and address, the detective flipped open his cell phone and began speaking in rapid Spanish. Less than a minute later, he hung up and turned back to Trey. "Your lady friend's car's outside waiting. I can have a courtesy car dropped off in less than ten minutes for you, Mr. Blackfox."

Trey gave a brief shake of this head. "No need, I've got another car at home." He turned toward Sasha. "Would you mind giving me a ride home?"

"Not at all."

As they exited the restaurant, Sasha asked, "So where exactly do you live?"

"South on Peachtree and west on Seventeenth, in midtown."

Sasha watched Trey from out of the corner of her eye as she pulled away from the restaurant. He gazed forlornly out the window. "Are you going to be all right?"

"Ask me that this time tomorrow."

"If you were having car problems I would have gladly picked you up."

Trey's pride, which had already taken a beating, let go of the ropes, and went down for the count. "The Range Rover's fine. The plan was for me to pick you up in Regan's Corvette, take you out to dinner and afterward a little tour of the city. I figured you wouldn't be able to resist my charms if I was driving a one-of-a-kind sports car."

She chuckled and his heart sped up. "I guess it's a good thing that I drove myself. I've always had a weakness for fast cars and handsome men."

"So you wait until I'm distracted to start flirting. That's pretty cruel when I'm contemplating being murdered by my little sister."

"You're telling me that your little sister drives a car that's barely street legal?"

"Our whole family has always been crazy about cars. Regan saved enough money to buy a used Corvette and then spent months refitting everything from the struts to the fuel intake. Not satisfied with just having the car, she started racing on weekends."

"I'm impressed."

"I am, too. She's good." He took a deep breath. "I've got to get that car back."

"You will. Something tells me that Frank won't stop until the car's back in your hands."

When they arrived at the address, Sasha slowed the car and couldn't help but scan the surroundings. She hadn't known what to expect, but it wasn't an ultra-modern condominium high-rise, a two-acre lake with green space on one block and retail district complete with upscale restaurants on the other.

"There's a supermarket, gourmet bakery, ice cream stop and video store around the corner," he said. "If you get a hankering for a midnight snack, want to catch a movie premiere or watch an old movie in bed, just let me know."

Sasha parked the car in the first available parking space in the underground garage. "Well, we're here."

"Care to honor a dying man's last wish and have a cup of coffee with me?"

She looked at him, leaned back in the passenger side, his brow furrowed, his eyes dark with worry. How could she not accept his request? "When you put it that way how can I refuse?"

They exited the sedan and Trey came over to Sasha's side and put his arm around her. Sasha stuck her ungloved hands into her coat pockets and leaned into his warmth. They entered the building via automatic doors. It felt more like walking into a chic boutique hotel than a home. Soaring ceilings, metropolitan décor, marble floors, a lounge area with a plasma TV on the wall and a concierge who greeted Trey by name.

The elevator whisked them upward to the twenty-eighth floor, and he let her into one of the three doors in the hallway.

He grinned. "Welcome to *casa de Trey*. Feel free to take off anything you like and make yourself comfortable."

She smiled and unbuttoned her coat. "I'll just take off my coat for now."

"Let me help you with that."

Obligingly Sasha turned around and his hands deftly moved over her arms and to her shoulders. Her eyes focused on the room when he turned away. The open room let out high open ceilings and shining hardwood floors. A hint of vanilla perfumed the air. Her eyes roved over the perfectly positioned coordinated furniture and landed on the floor-to-ceiling windows on downtown and a wide Georgia sky. Sasha took a step forward, then stopped.

"What's wrong?" Trey paused from hanging her clothing in the closet.

She laughed, then bent down and began to pull off her heels. "I've crossed so many continents that I get confused. In Asia, it's shoes are off in the house. Some parts of Africa, no shoes period, and your feet would freeze without insulated boots during a Canadian winter."

"Never thought of that. So they really take their shoes off in Asia? I remember hearing about it when I was a kid, but I always thought the teacher was making it up."

"You've never traveled to Asia?"

Trey shook his head. "That's one of the many things I've been meaning to do. I haven't traveled much unless you count the Bahamas, Bermuda, Mexico and Canada."

"They count." She smiled. "Very nice place you have here."

"You sound surprised."

Sasha returned her attention to Trey and she once again noticed the way his clothes seemed to have been designed expressly for his physique and style. His shoes were of excellent quality, his socks always matched and his hair was precisely cut. This man knew how to take care of himself. If Sasha had been paying more attention with her head instead of her hormones, she would have expected his home to be in the same condition.

She waved her hand at the nice artwork. "Most men I know have eclectic decorating themes in their houses with college furniture alongside Italian leather recliners, and others have the bare minimum of a chair and a big-screen home entertainment unit."

She nodded her head towards the open living room. "However, you have a designer's jewel here. Did you pick out everything yourself?"

"No, I had plenty of help getting the loft into shape. I found the place about three months before it was set to be finished. My real estate agent actually had to camp out in the lobby for the management office to open on the first day of the sale. Then after we inked the deal and my mother drove down, hired a contractor, decorators and a bunch of people. I actually didn't even see the finished product until the night of my house warming party."

"That's convenient."

"Not when you walk into your bathroom and find half the countertop decorated with designer perfume bottles and gender-neutral stuffed animals in the guest closet. It's my mother's idea of a hint."

Sasha laughed playfully. "Somehow I think you got off lightly. Your mother didn't strike me as the kind of woman who beats around the bush when there's something she wants."

"Very true. Now, how about I give you a quick tour of the place?"

The living and dining rooms on the main level were open to high ceilings and lofty exposed ductwork. In the living area a slender large screen television served as the focal point of a black leather sofa, love seat, recliner and ottoman flanked with matching end tables and sleek modern lamps. Sasha glanced at the coffee table and was encouraged to see evidence that Trey actually lived in the loft. Scattered papers and veterinary journals lay atop the coffee table. A small door led into an office. Off the dining room, a walk-out through sliding glass doors led to a charming, secluded balcony. A breakfast bar complete with elevated wooden stools separated the dining room from the kitchen. "Nice kitchen."

"My mother said the decorator called it the 'bachelor special.'"

Trey put his hand on the indoor grill. "Since we aren't allowed to grill on the balconies, this was my only request."

Sasha ran her finger over the island countertop and looked at the empty sink. The center island with its granite countertop, stainless steel double sink, and chrome-plated faucets could have been installed yesterday. "How long have you lived here?"

"About a year."

She shook her head. "Did the maid come today or yesterday? This place is too clean to be true."

"You haven't seen everything yet."

"So she came yesterday."

"Nope. Last week. I have someone come in every other week and give the place a good cleaning. Other than that, I do a decent job of not messing up the place. And just so I can spoil the perfect image you have of me, I'll show you the upstairs."

The rest of the loft included two bedrooms, two baths. Sasha was almost overjoyed to see a few socks and boxer shorts on the master suite's floor. An unmade king-size bed sat in the center of the bedroom. The bathrooms had white cultured-marble countertops, porcelain tile flooring, a separate shower stall with a framed glass door and a five-foot step-in tub. Even the laundry area was spacious and neatly decorated with built-in shelves.

Trey guided Sasha downstairs and pulled out a barstool. "Have a seat while I get everything ready."

"So where's the automatic part?" Sasha asked after placing her elbows on the breakfast bar and resting her chin in her hands. Before leaving the restaurant, he'd mentioned that the coffee would be ready when they arrived at his house.

Trey reached into the cherry wood cabinets and pulled out two cups. "Well, it was a half truth. The machine is automatic but it won't start brewing until six tomorrow morning."

She tilted her head to the side and smiled. "So you lied."

"In a way. But once you try one of my cappuccinos you won't remember anything."

"Can I help?"

"How about you reach into the fridge and grab the milk. This thing can steam and froth."

"I guess I should have expected the perfect gourmet kitchen to include a coffee bar."

"Hey, I like my toys."

Trey added cold water into the machine, then after using the espresso grinder, firmly pressed the tamper to pack and level the coffee grind in the filter handle. It took less than thirty seconds to produce the single shot of dark liquid. Next, he topped both cups with equal parts of steamed, frothy milk and a sprinkle of chocolate powder. When he was finished, he took both of the mugs into the living room and sat them on the coffee table.

Sasha sat next to him on the couch. She added sugar to her mug and stirred. She held the cup to her nose and inhaled. She closed her eyes as the scent evoked images of an April morning in Vienna when she'd sat with friends at a small café on the town's main street. Unbidden, a soft smile grew on her face as she took a sip of the creamy liquid. The cappuccino was wonderful. She opened her eyes and glanced at Trey. "You know I probably shouldn't be drinking cappuccino so late in the evening. I might not be able to sleep tonight."

"I know a couple of ways to burn off the caffeine."

"And what would those happen to be?"

"First, there's the one in my dreams, and the other's on the thirteenth floor."

Sasha sidestepped the mention of his dreams. She'd had her fair share of R-rated dreams since he'd kissed her. Every time she walked into the greenhouse, Sasha had a flashback. Somehow without her knowing it, the veterinarian had gotten under her skin and every moment they were together would make it increasingly difficult to forget about him. "What's on the thirteenth floor that could help me sleep tonight?"

"The amenity centre. It has a fitness room with TVs, showers, saunas and a Jacuzzi." He shrugged. "I haven't checked it out yet so we can always go for a late-night visit."

"Then how do you do it?"

"What?"

She pointed her spoon at him. "I've touched your stomach, Trey. You don't have the body of a man who drinks cappuccinos and sits behind a desk."

"Besides hauling around fifty-pound canines, I'm an outdoor kind of guy. I either do laps around the pond or run in Piedmont Park. When it gets too cold or when basketball season starts up again, I'll head downstairs. Nothing like cheering your team on and getting a good run in at the same time."

"Do they allow pets here?"

"For the price of this place, they allow anything you want."

"And yet you don't have any pets?"

"No, I'm really never at home. I wouldn't want to keep a dog cooped up in here all day and half the night waiting for me to come home."

"Good point. I'm not sure what I would do if Jackson wasn't around. I still get a little nervous feeding the iguana."

"It's the way they cock their heads to the side and stare at you, right?" He laughed. "Sometimes I have flashbacks to the day my brother snuck me in to see *Godzilla* on opening night."

Sasha leaned forward and put her coffee mug on the table as laughter tickled her throat. "You said it. I know she's not dangerous, but I'm still happy that she has her space and I have mine."

"Exactly," Trey agreed.

Sasha sighed. "Speaking of pets, I need to go.

An Important Message from the Publisher

Dear Reader,

Because you've chosen to read one of our fine novels, I'd like to say "thank you"! And, as a special way to say thank you, I'm offering to send you two more Kimani Romance novels and two surprise gifts – absolutely FREE! These books will keep it real with true-to-life African American characters that turn up the heat and sizzle with passion.

Please enjoy the free books and gifts with our compliments...

Linda Gill

Publisher, Kimani Press

Peel off Seal and Place Inside...

Two NEW Kimani Romance™ Novels
Two exciting surprise gifts

I have placed my
Editor's "thank you" Free Gifts
seal in the space provided at
right. Please send me 2 FREE
books, and my 2 FREE Mystery
Gifts. I understand that I am
under no obligation to purchase
anything further, as explained on
the back of this card.

**PLACE
FREE GIFTS
SEAL
HERE**

168 XDL EF2P   368 XDL EF2Z

FIRST NAME	LAST NAME

ADDRESS

APT.#	CITY

STATE/PROV.	ZIP/POSTAL CODE

Thank You!

The Reader Service — Here's How It Works:

BUSINESS REPLY MAIL

FIRST-CLASS MAIL   PERMIT NO. 717-003   BUFFALO, NY

POSTAGE WILL BE PAID BY ADDRESSEE

THE READER SERVICE
3010 WALDEN AVE
PO BOX 1867
BUFFALO NY 14240-9952

NO POSTAGE
NECESSARY
IF MAILED
IN THE
UNITED STATES

If offer card is missing write to: The Reader Service, 3010 Walden Ave., P.O. Box 1867, Buffalo, NY 14240-1867

Remember I've got a spoiled cat, hyperactive dog, some frogs and an iguana at home waiting for me."

Trey stood and held out a hand that she took without thinking. "Let me walk you to your car."

After a quick ride down in the elevator, they came to a stop in front of her car. "You sure you can find your way home? I can follow you," he volunteered.

"I just need to jump on and off the interstate. I'll be fine."

"Call me when you get in?"

"I'm a big girl, Trey. I can take care of myself."

"Do it for me. I'd like one less thing to worry about disappearing tonight."

"I'm sorry," she reached out and touched his cheek. In the easy niceness of the evening, she'd forgotten about the stolen car. "I'm sure they'll find it."

"From your beautiful lips to God's ears."

He took her hand, turned her wrist toward his mouth and placed a kiss there before she could speak. His eyes were as dark as chocolate, and Sasha stared mesmerized as he leaned close. She didn't have time to draw a breath before he kissed her.

His kiss tasted like coffee and cream, smooth with the lingering taste of chicory. Trey's lips were gentle and curious. When he deepened the kiss, she reached up and placed her hands on his arms, feeling the solid tight muscle. She closed her eyes and concentrated on the feeling. She tasted the warmth of him and licked the lingering sweetness from his lips. She opened her mouth and their tongues engaged in a courtship dance, touching, dancing, darting. She wrapped her arms around his waist to balance, bringing her into close contact with hard evidence of his state of arousal. When he lifted his mouth and broke the kiss, she was breathless, dizzy and hungry for more. Sasha dropped her head against Trey's chest and inhaled.

"You really don't have to go home," he murmured. His chin rested against the top of her head.

"Yes, I do," Sasha murmured, touching her finger to her lips.

"I knew you would say that."

Sasha drew back and lifted her brows. "Then why did you ask?"

His lips curled in a grin as he opened the driver's side door. "I've never been particularly lucky, but I thought what the heck. Maybe I might catch one break tonight."

"Not tonight."

"How about Friday night? I can open a bottle of wine, fix a nice dinner—"

Sasha interrupted, "I'm not going to have sex with you on Friday night, either, Trey."

He held up his hands and his dark eyes twinkled with amusement. "I want you bad enough that my teeth ache, sweetness, but if you'd have let me finish, I was about to say we could watch a movie."

Her glare didn't affect his enjoyment of her discomfort in the slightest. Sasha got into the car and went to grab her seat belt, but Trey beat her to it. She stared straight ahead and only managed to let a small gasp escape as his hand brushed across her breast.

"I'll see you Thursday morning at eleven," he said, and laughed as he walked back toward the building.

She took a deep breath, let it out slowly, and put the key into the ignition. Lord, she had it bad. The kind of bad that had her forgetting important things like Trey's commitment-phobic past and her own unknown future.

The next morning Trey cleared his throat after rinsing off his toothbrush. "Regan…" He stopped. For the past three hours, he'd stared at his cell phone as the sun rose. "Little sister, you remember that time when you were eight?"

He stared into the mirror and tried to make his lips curl upward in a carefree smile. "Yeah, you remember the day I borrowed your Tonka toy? The red one that could go on water and I accidentally lost it in the creek?"

He pictured his little sister, Regan, nodding her head. "Well, after you cried for a little bit, I got you a nice new one, remember. Remember that you didn't cry anymore? You kept that Tonka toy until we got those new bikes for Christmas."

"Well, I know you're wondering why I'm telling you this." He paused and drew in a deep breath. "Because, surprise, I got you a brand-new top-of-the-line Corvette. This baby will be custom designed from the factory in

Detroit. I'm having the rims special made at the same place that caters to all the music stars." Trey picked up his toothbrush. Nah, that won't work, he thought to himself.

He pulled out the toothpaste from behind the mirrored cabinet. "Regan, I've got good news and I've got bad. Oh, you want the bad first. All right then, a valet at a restaurant took your Corvette and forgot to bring it back. Wait—wait. The good news is that I went online and bought you a new one last night."

Trey put down the toothbrush and looked in the mirror. Man, he couldn't believe this crap. Regan would tear him to shreds. His little sister had rebuilt that car. She knew that Corvette like the back of her hand and had raced it more times than he could count. The thought settled in his stomach along with the filet mignon he'd consumed a mere ten hours before.

In his mind, he went through all the possibilities, including writing a letter or asking his mother to break the news. Regan was dating an artist and riding the wave of family popularity. This mess would definitely get him kicked into the doghouse and he had zero confidence that the Corvette would be found before his deadline to return it.

Man, he should have trusted his instincts and parked the car himself, but last night he'd had only one thing on his mind: Sasha. She was still on his mind. That kiss last night just cemented what he knew. Sex with her would be incredible. He went rock hard just thinking about it. Trey put down his toothbrush, turned on the facet, and splashed cold water over his face. A quick glance at his watch told him everything he needed to know. Thirty-two hours and counting, he thought. Either he'd be sitting behind the wheel of Regan's Corvette, or he'd be enjoying one last evening before a nasty confession.

Chapter 9

The next morning Trey picked up the phone and heard a masculine voice say, "Good morning, Dr. Blackfox. This is the concierge and there's a gentleman here who needs you to sign for an automobile delivery."

"Be down in two minutes," he said, and then slammed down the phone.

He jumped out of bed and threw on the first thing he could find in his closet. It wasn't until the elevator doors closed that he realized he'd put on two different colored socks and high-water jeans. He shook his hand and frantically pressed the button for the ground floor. Relieved that the detective had managed to locate Regan's car, he had no idea of the car's condition. If the thief had taken the car to a chop shop, it would be impossible for him to replace the parts before he had to return the Corvette to his little sister.

When the elevator doors opened, Trey flew across the lobby and through the automatic glass doors. His knees weakened at the sight of Regan's car atop the flatbed truck. He walked over just as a man stepped out of the driver's side.

"Are you Trey Blackfox?"

"Yes."

"Got some ID?"

He reached for his back pocket and realized that he'd left everything in the loft, including his keys. "I left it upstairs."

"Well, I need to see your license before I can release the car."

"No problem. I'll go back and get it. But can you tell me if anything was taken?"

"Car looks fine. The man who arranged for delivery even handed over the keys."

"Was he about my height, dark-skinned, bald head and could have doubled for a professional boxer?"

"Yep. That sounds like the man. Look, it's nice talking with you and all, but it's cold out here and I have a few more pick-ups and deliveries today."

Trey nodded and smiled as relief flooded through his body. "I'll be right back with my license," he said aloud, but mentally added, "And you can have all the cash I have in my wallet." He grinned as he strode through the doors. His luck was back. Now all he had to do was win Sasha Clayton over.

Three hours later, after a quick tour of the outside exhibits, Trey drew Sasha to a stop in front of a closed portion of the zoo.

"'Future home of the Golden Lion tamarins,'" Sasha read the overhead banner aloud.

"With your help, this facility will become one of a group of national zoos conducting research to better understand the process of reintroduction of the tamarins into the rainforest."

Sasha shook her head. "I appreciate the thought, Trey, but you have the wrong person. My research has primarily focused on four-legged mammals. I don't have much experience with primates."

"But you do have firsthand knowledge of the Brazilian rainforest. You spent the two years there."

"I was in the middle of the forest. If I'm not mistaken the tamarins are native to a forest near Rio de Janiero."

"You're right, and the zoo brought in representatives from the Brazilian primate centre to help with the design, training and environment recommendations. They've got a fully funded team dedicated to care for the exhibit, which will include this indoor space and mixed species, free range wooded area."

Sasha surveyed the area. "It sounds like a good plan, but I'm not sure I can help you with this."

"We're just looking for another pair of eyes and ears, Sasha."

She rubbed the bridge of her nose. "It's not because I don't feel as though I have nothing to contribute. I just feel that we don't have the right to keep animals in captivity."

"We're going to try to make the exhibit as similar to their natural environment as possible."

"It's still not the same," she insisted. "How can you simulate the call of the birds in the morning? How can you copy the fog rising over the canopy at daylight or the downpour of the summer rains?"

He stepped closer to her. "This is a chance to save this species from extinction."

"They're almost extinct because of humankind."

"And you have the chance to help turn it around. The goal here is not only to help repopulate the species but to also show our generation and the next how to be better stewards of the environment." He placed his finger under her chin and forced eye contact. The sight of her lovely brown eyes made his heart skip a beat. "This exhibit is to show people what they'll miss if they don't support conservation efforts like this."

"I've spent my entire life observing animals in the wild, Trey. It's not a simple thing you're asking me to support."

"But it's the right thing, Sasha. Your godfather felt the same way," he said.

"Uncle Camden was involved in this?"

"He funded over a quarter of the exhibit."

Sasha gently pulled her hands from Trey and walked over to the side of the plastic window and sighed. "I'll need a little time."

"So you're not turning me down completely?"

She smiled a little. "Is that possible?"

"If you were my mother it would be a requirement."

"How is she?"

"Happily planning my grandfather's birthday celebration."

"You sound pleased."

He laughed. "I'm not the only one. My brothers are breathing easier now that she has something to distract her from planning their lives."

"Sounds serious."

Trey nodded. "It is. Before she and my father retired, Mom was head of the company's project planning office. The family jokes that if it's not on Rose's plan, then it won't happen."

They walked along an outside path. Sasha chuckled. "Your mother sounds a lot like mine. I learned everything I needed to know about planning an expedition just by watching her work. My father would be lost without her."

"Same for my family. All of the family businesses are headed by Blackfox men, but without our women for support, we'd never make it."

"It's not that often you hear high praise like that."

He shrugged his shoulders. "Ask anybody in the

family and they'll tell you the same thing." He chuckled. "It's well known that you can mess with Blackfox money, but you can't mess with our women."

Surprisingly Trey's words struck a strong chord in her heart. It didn't erase the small fact that he had the traits of a borderline womanizer, and the paternalistic overtones of his family rankled her independent nature, but his respectful manner did make her look upon him in an increasingly better light. Before she said or did something she might regret, Sasha returned her attention to the zoo grounds. "So where to next?"

He reached over, placed his arm around the small of Sasha's back, and pulled her in close. "Just thought I'd round out the tour with a stop in our last indoor exhibit."

Enjoying the sudden warmth of Trey's body, Sasha relaxed and smiled up at him. "And what's in there?"

"Some of my favorites—spiders, snakes and a few praying mantises."

Ten minutes later after what he'd thought would be a perfect ending to a relaxing afternoon, Trey's heart stopped as he turned toward Sasha. He didn't stop because of the soft smile on her face as she examined the exhibit's ladybugs. "You know, maybe not all bugs are bad. These are actually cute."

"Sasha, don't move," he said calmly.

Her smile dimmed. "Trey, what's wrong?"

"Honey." He put the emphasis in his voice and took off his jacket. The sight of the yellow-and-dark-striped scorpion crawling up the back of her coat stopped his heart. The closer the scorpion got to her exposed neck, the greater the chance it might sting her.

"Just don't move."

"What's wrong?" she asked again, her voice rose in pitch.

"There's a scorpion on your back."

"Did you just say there's a scorpion on my back?"

"Yes. Now I know you won't panic, right?" He took a baby step forward.

"I hate scorpions, Trey. I have a phobia," she nearly screamed. "Get it off me."

"When I count to three I want you to leap forward. I'm going to knock it off."

"What if it bites?"

"Just do it, Sasha. One."

Adrenaline kicked into overtime. "Two...three."

She moved; he swatted the damn thing. Trey sprinted to the closest trash bin and quickly dumped it in and tied the garbage bag. He'd just finished tying a double knot when he heard a thump.

Trey turned and discovered Sasha crumpled on the ground.

"Damn it," he cursed and sprinted over to kneel by her side. He quickly checked her pulse and found it steady. For a split second, he considered going for help, but he didn't want to leave her alone. "Sasha...Sasha." He gently stroked her face and whispered, "Wake up, beautiful. The scorpion is gone."

"Trey." Her eyes opened unfocused. "What happened? Where's the scorpion?"

"You're safe. He's in the garbage bag over there. Now how are you feeling?"

She drew a deep breath before answering, "I'm fine."

He stared at her incredulously. The woman had just fainted onto the floor not more than three minutes ago. When she attempted to pull out of his lap, Trey held her still. "No, you're not. You're pulse is rapid and I'm surprised you haven't started to hyperventilate."

"Okay, Trey." She swung her head around to face him. "I'm not all right. And I won't be okay until I get out of this room."

"One of the directors is out of town for the week. I'll take you to his office and you can rest on the sofa."

With his hands underneath her arms, Trey helped Sasha stand. Even when they were both back on their feet, she stood close to him. His arm found its way around her back and she fit perfectly next to him. He'd started out wanting to impress the woman, but had almost gotten her stung by a scorpion. He shouldn't have brought her into the exhibit.

The slight trembling of her hands tightened his teeth with recrimination. No doubt he'd been frozen with fear when he'd seen it. Trey tried to remember the last time he'd experienced the gut-wrenching sensation and couldn't find the answer. Not one to ponder long, he pushed his train of thought aside. After he'd gotten them out of the building and halfway to the administrative offices, he asked, "Why didn't you tell me that you're afraid of insects?"

"Because I'm not."

"Sasha, you just fainted."

She placed her hands in her pockets. "I'm not afraid of insects. I've been crawled on by more of them than I care to remember. But I was bitten by a scorpion as a child. I know what it feels like and the thought of having that happen again…" Her voice trailed off into a whisper, and then she reached up and wiped her eyes.

"And yet you still were next to the cage?"

"My career is based on wildlife research. There are scorpions and things that are worse than scorpions out there in the jungle. If I let the fear get to me, I won't be able to conduct my research."

"Sounds like you're ready to get back to work."

"Not yet. For the moment, Jackson volunteered to continue helping me with Uncle Camden's pets until I can find a replacement. And I really don't want to find someone else. I like being woken up with Zaza curled on the bottom of the bed and I feel like a kid again when I play fetch with Darwin."

Trey opened the door for Sasha and they entered into the zoo's office building. "Wait here for a moment, so I can tell someone what happened and they can go put your deadly admirer friend back in his cage."

"You're funny."

He flashed a big grin and was gratified to see a ghost

of a smile on Sasha's lips. "What can I say, the little thing had good taste. He saw a beautiful woman and just wanted to get a little closer."

She rolled her eyes toward the ceiling, and then waved him away. "Go. I'll wait here."

Five minutes later after he'd dispatched one of the zoo keepers to go and take care of his wayward charge, he let them both into the director's empty office. "Can I get you something to drink?"

"No, thank you." She sat down on the sofa. "I think that little scorpion incident is a sign that I shouldn't take on this project."

"That was an accident. The tapir habitat is on the opposite side of the zoo."

Sasha tilted her face and rested her cheek on the palm of her hand.

"To be honest, I haven't thought of this as helping the zoo. I've only thought of it as helping you."

He sat in opposite of the couch. "If that gets us the help we need than, please help me."

"That's the problem. I doubt that I can handle this by myself. I've approached Jackson about continuing his role as the animal's caregiver and estate manager. But honestly, I don't expect him to stay on. Why would he want to? He was Uncle Camden's best friend and now he's financially set. He could retire tomorrow if he wanted to."

"But he might stay out of loyalty to your godfather."

"Exactly. I don't know how I can do this without him, Trey. The attorneys, accountants and bankers manage a lot of things, but I'm still floundering. It's hard enough to manage my checkbook and a project budget." She sighed. "Lord, I'm tired of hearing myself whine."

"Well, I don't mind listening."

"Sure."

He stood and took a seat next to Sasha on the sofa. "I'm serious. In fact I find this conversation fascinating. Most women I know would be on a plane to Milan for retail therapy. Yet you're here trying to find a way to get back to the edge of civilization."

"You're not going to let me feel sorry for myself, are you?"

"Not today. We need you here at the zoo and you need a new focus. It's a win-win situation."

"What's in this for you, Trey? Why are you pushing this zoo project so hard?"

"Truth?"

"Truth." She looked him dead in the eyes.

Trey racked his brain to come up something as she sat back and folded her arms underneath her bosom, making her hint of cleavage irresistible to his eyes. In the beginning there had been only one thing on his mind when he'd come up with the idea of approaching Sasha with the project, and he couldn't tell her that yet. He pulled his gaze upwards and his dilemma went from bad to worse as those beautifully discerning eyes and pouting lips jumpstarted his libido.

He leaned back against the armrest and managed a grin. "I don't think you can handle the truth."

She narrowed her eyes. "I think you're stalling."

He shrugged. "My motives for wanting you to help won't matter if you're hell-bent on leaving town."

"I'm not leaving town until I feel confident that Uncle Camden's wishes have been met."

"All right. Then you can help us out until then. Sasha, we're this close to being accepted into a national breeding program. If we can add your name and credentials to the proposal, we'll have the tapir exhibit set up with a small population before the end of the year."

"You won't give this up, will you?"

"Nope," he grinned. "When I was growing up my mother would give us a new dictionary word every day. Once after I refused to eat liver, she called me obstinate and made me look up the word in the dictionary and write it a hundred times. Personally I don't see it. I think I'm a big pushover. Now my brother, Marius, he's more stubborn than my grandfather's old mule Gracie."

"I've heard that stubbornness is a genetic personality trait inherent in males," she reasoned.

Just then, the door swung open and someone entered the room "Trey, Mike told me that a scorpion got loose and attacked a visitor."

Sasha recognized the voice in an instant and stood

up as old memories came flooding back into her consciousness.

The visitor stopped in his tracks and his eyes widened. "Sasha?"

She smiled and held out her hands. "Kenneth."

He strode toward her and instead of taking her hands engulfed her in a big hug. "What are you doing here? No, that's not important. You're the visitor that was almost bitten, aren't you?"

Sasha tried to speak but couldn't with her face pressed tightly against the side of Kenneth's sport coat.

"Are you alright?" he asked after a moment. He relaxed his grip yet still held her arms.

"I'm fine," she stated for the tenth time in the past half hour. "I don't know if *attack* is the right word. Let's just say he got a little too close for comfort," she replied ruefully.

"Did it sting?"

"No. Trey managed to get it off me."

Kenneth took her hand within his. "I'm surprised you were in the exhibit. I thought you hated bugs."

Annoyed with being ignored, Trey stood up. "I take it that introductions are unnecessary?"

"Sasha and I went to graduate school together."

"I thought you went to business school," Trey responded.

"I did. The veterinary school was right across the walk. We met at an on-campus mixer. It's been over five years but even after all this time, you look lovely."

"Thank you."

"Are you busy? I was going to head out for lunch before an afternoon meeting. Why don't we grab something to eat and catch up?"

Sasha started to answer, but Trey spoke first. "Sorry, Kenneth, but I've got to get back to the clinic and I've got a few things to run by Sasha before I leave."

Kenneth reached into his pocket and pulled out a business card, and laid it in Sasha's hand. "Promise me you'll call today."

"I promise."

"It's great seeing you again, girl." The man leaned in and gave her a kiss on the cheek.

Trey stood up and kept the smile on his face until he'd managed to close the door behind Kenneth. When he turned around and relaxed his face, he thought his face might crack from the release of effort it had taken him to keep a neutral expression.

He'd never thought of himself as the jealous type. He dated his fair share of women who'd carried the trait and until he'd learned to give out an upfront disclaimer that he had no plans of making any woman in his life the next Mrs. Blackfox, they'd made his personal life a textbook case of drama. Yet, when Kenneth had pulled Sasha close and kissed her on the cheek, he'd wanted to smash his fist into the man's jaw.

"Old friend?" He sat down again in his chair and frowned.

"Sometimes. Depends on the situation."

"And how would you find the situation you're in now?"

She rubbed her brow with her fingers and sat back on the sofa. "Very awkward. That's how I would define this, Trey."

"That wasn't exactly the kind of answer I was looking for."

"Then tell me what you're looking for, Trey. Help me figure out what's going on between us." She waved a hand in his direction. "If there is something between us."

Trey didn't even deign to answer her statement with a verbal response. Instead he pushed out of his seat and before she could open her mouth, he'd pinned Sasha to the couch with his arms on both sides and crushed his lips with hers. He slanted his mouth over hers and didn't wait for an invitation; he demanded it and when her lips yielded against his and the hands that had seconds before pushed against his chest clutched his sweater, Trey wanted to shout his triumph. Instead, he wrapped his hands about her back and pulled her closer, pressing her breasts against his chest.

The second he pulled away, she touched her fingertips to her lips. And he kept his eyes locked with hers. Finally after several moments passed. He spoke. "Tell me there's no fire and I'll call you the worst liar the world has ever seen."

She cut her eyes to the side. "Point taken."

"Good. Now, before I move on to my second point, I need to know about Kenneth."

"There's really nothing to know. We dated in college."

"Was it a clean break?"

"As clean as parental politics can make it. His parents didn't approve of me or the relationship. My blood wasn't blue enough and my family's bank account wasn't high enough to meet their standards."

"So if it wasn't for his parents you might still be together?"

"No. We probably would have broken up sooner or later. Kenneth is more of the corporate type. I don't think he would have been able to deal the long distance relationship my job would have entailed."

"Well, the situation's changed now."

"What's changed?"

"You're going to be in Atlanta for a while and you've got a large bank account."

"You're only half-right. I may have money, which still doesn't feel like it's my own. But I haven't changed to the point that I could be naive enough to think that Kenneth and I could get back together."

"Glad to hear that."

Sasha stood up and pulled on her coat. "You shouldn't. Just because I'm attracted to you, Trey, doesn't mean that I'm going to get mixed up with you."

"Too late. We're already involved and I'm looking forward to taking this new relationship to deeper levels."

"We'll see," Sasha replied over her shoulder. "I'll call you about the project."

Trey didn't miss the challenge inherent in her voice. If he was going to set the record straight, he had to do it now. "I'll drop by and get the good news in person."

Chapter 10

Sasha had spent most of Wednesday fuming about what a jerk Trey had been, and Thursday wasn't much better. It didn't help that he kept dropping by the house to check on Darwin's condition and stare at her like she had broken all of the Ten Commandments by agreeing to have lunch with Kenneth.

It didn't help that she'd started to run out of excuses as to why she hadn't told her parents about her inheritance and her semi-permanent relocation to Atlanta. Worst of all, she felt guilty. She wished she hadn't accepted Kenneth's lunch invitation. She didn't want to reminisce about the past. She wanted to forget about everything and curl up in bed with a pint of ice cream, an old movie or a good book.

"Did I tell you how stunning you look, Sasha?" Kenneth said in a voice that would have had raised goose bumps on her skin any other day.

Sasha sighed inwardly. They'd only been seated at the nearby country club's dining room for ten minutes, but she already wanted to run back to her car. "Yes, you mentioned it after finding me passed out in Trey's office the other day. Kenneth, why are you staring at me like we've never met?"

She closed her menu and looked at him. Not that it didn't feel good to have such a handsome man staring at her like a bear just out of hibernation. She recognized the look because Trey had stared at her that same way before he'd kissed her. The thought alone brought her hand to the water glass to drink a gulp of the liquid. She needed to stop thinking about Trey. But her mind had other ideas as it flashed back to that night.

If only the veterinarian's sexy dimple and broad shoulders didn't send her hormones into overdrive. She was too old have a case of adolescent infatuation, and too smart to not believe fire burned. She took a deep breath and held it for several heartbeats. Trey Blackfox had the earmarking of a raging wildfire. Pushing the notion aside, she returned her attention to Kenneth.

He shook his head. "It's just that I never expected to see you again and to see you now is very disconcerting."

"In what way?"

"I was just thinking about us last week. Or thinking

about you. I went back to the university for an alumni conference and as I walked across the main lawn I remembered all the times we sat on an old blanket and watched the sunset," he said.

Sasha couldn't help but smile at the memory. Too bad they could only have done it three times before discovering that Kenneth had a violent allergic reaction to ragweed. "We had good times and bad times."

"More good than bad, I hope," he replied.

"I wouldn't be here if it hadn't been."

"The world keeps getting smaller." He smiled. "I'm going to have to buy Trey a beer for bringing you to the zoo. So how did the two of you meet anyway?"

"He's helping me out with some pets that I've recently inherited."

Kenneth shook head from side to side. "Sometimes I wonder how he does it. Trey manages a thriving vet practice, consults for the zoo and juggles a harem of women."

"Good time management, I suppose," she replied dryly.

"It doesn't hurt to have a silver spoon," Kenneth laughed. "Then again, it works for me."

"So you're saying that Trey's a self-centered trust fund baby, too?" Outwardly, it sounded as if she was teasing. Inwardly, Sasha was serious. It wasn't as if this were a normal situation. Here she was about to have lunch with her ex-flame, but talking about the man who had her hormones in an uproar. That piece of the truth almost made Sasha drop her elbows on the table.

"That's harsh."

She waved a hand. "If the shoe fits…"

"You'll have to ask him about the size of his trust. My guess is it's eight figures."

Sasha did the calculation in her head and the number of zeros sunk like lead in her stomach. She'd been under the impression that he'd grown up in a middle class home just by the way he spoke, the way he dressed, the loft and his vehicle. But the thought that he could be a millionaire hadn't crossed her mind.

Inwardly she sighed. As if she needed another reason she shouldn't get involved with Trey. Maybe she was cursed. She had to be the only woman who didn't want to date or mate a man with more money than he could spend in a few lifetimes.

"I'll try to remember to ask."

"So what have you really been doing since school? I've heard rumors about you joining some radical conservation group and living in caves in Ecuador."

"I worked on an internationally funded research project in Honduras, but I'm not a member of any group except for the Royal Science Academy in the UK."

"Congratulations."

"Thank you."

"So now you're back in the U.S.? Settling down at last?"

"Not really," she responded, and then turned the conversation back in Kenneth's direction. "But from the looks of it, you've managed to get out from under your father's thumb."

He laughed. "Not completely. I still have to go to the management meetings, and help out with the firm's public relations. But I'm lucky that Daniel wanted to run the business."

"That's a surprise to hear. Your mother practically had Future CEO carved into your bronzed baby shoes."

He laughed. "You're not kidding. I threw my baby brother the party of the century after he got his MBA and started working under Dad."

"Kenneth!" a high-pitched voice unexpectedly called out from across the dining room. Heads turned toward the entryway and many of the diners followed the progress of the stranger who was making a straight line toward their table.

Sasha's radar went up and the sister who was dressed in a pinstriped suit strolled over to the table. She was model thin with few curves and long legs. Her long curly hair was pulled back into a ponytail. Her caramel-brown skin was unblemished and her make-up stopped short of a work of art. She flashed a bright smile and held up a diamond-covered wrist.

She watched her ex-boyfriend stand; his wide smile didn't hide uneasy eyes.

"Kenneth, darling, what a surprise to see you here. Why didn't you tell me you were coming for lunch? I would have rescheduled my tennis lesson and joined you."

"Arabella, what a surprise," he replied, not as warmly as the woman who'd come to a stop next to their table. She snuggled into his chest, wrapped her arms around his stomach and then kissed his cheek.

"I didn't expect to see you at the country club."

She drew back in surprise. "How could you not? You know I have tennis lessons on Wednesday and Monika and I play a set on Thursday."

"Sorry to disappoint you, but keeping up with your schedule isn't high on my priority list."

"That wasn't nice. You're sounding more and more like Daddy everyday."

The newcomer stood upright and tall, feet spread shoulder length apart. She was small and had great muscle tone and she had a smooth complexion a pre-teen would envy. Her long black ponytail and dainty facial features reminded Sasha of a Barbie doll.

She's beautiful and she knows it. Sasha picked up her glass to hide the amused look on her face as Arabella sported what had to have been the biggest pout she'd ever seen and Kenneth's face froze.

"Not now, Arabella. As you can see, I have company."

"That you haven't introduced. How rude of you, darling."

"Arabella Lamar." She held out her hand.

"Sasha Clayton," she replied. She passed on her best

smile and extended her hand. Arabella wore wealth and privilege like a badge of honor. Her attitude of ownership over Kenneth rankled Sasha's last nerve. She wasn't romantically interested in her ex. She hadn't been for long time. But just because she wasn't aiming for Kenneth didn't mean she was going to let this little barracuda treat her like dirt.

"Sasha. Have we met? I thought I knew all of Kenneth's colleagues at the zoo."

"No, I don't work at the zoo."

"For the moment," Kenneth replied. "I'm hoping to lure Sasha on-board to help design and manage the new tapir habitat."

"Well, you might as well go ahead and accept. Kenneth here is relentless when he wants something."

"Yes, I remember how persuasive he can be," she dryly replied. The only time he didn't get his way with was his father, she thought.

Arabella blinked and looked back and forth between the two of them. Seconds ago, her eyes had been wider than a baby gazelle; now the orbs narrowed into slits. "You know each other?"

Sasha opened her mouth to respond. "Kenneth and I were—"

"College sweethearts," he finished.

Sasha barely forced herself not to glare at Kenneth as he sat at the table oblivious to the awkward position he'd just placed her in.

"Really. How nice."

Sasha blinked twice at the obvious lie and rushed to lessen the impact of Kenneth's statement. "We haven't seen each other since graduation. I had no idea he'd settled in Atlanta."

"What a coincidence. So where are you coming from?"

"Everywhere. I'm a wildlife researcher so I've been traveling a lot. I rent a studio apartment in New York so that I can store things and have an address to put on all of my travel documents."

"And you'll be moving here to Atlanta?"

"I'm here on personal business and I'll remain here until that's resolved. After that I'm not sure."

The waiter took that moment to bring their orders and Sasha was about to release an internal sigh of relief until she spied Arabella's pinched mouth. She busied herself rearranging her napkin in an attempt to politely ignore the furious exchange of whispers between the couple.

"Bella, we'll talk later, okay?" said Kenneth loudly.

Somehow she managed a bright smile, but her eyes could have been reclassified as a lethal weapon. "Of course. I'll be over after seven."

One peck on the cheek and she was gone. Sasha waited until she'd cleared the room before speaking. "Telling her we were college sweethearts wasn't the smartest move you've ever made."

He smiled, and then reached out for the bottle of ketchup. "I might regret it later, but that felt good. Arabella can be a spoiled brat."

"She must have some redeeming qualities if you're dating her."

"No kidding. She's great on the eyes, and has connections to all the key players in Atlanta. Her father's a shoo-in for the senate elections next year, and she's a tiger in bed." He grimaced. "If only she kept quiet and stop trying to run my life she'd be perfect."

Sasha almost choked on her French fry. After politely wiping off her mouth, she shook her head. "T.M.I., Kenneth. Way too much information."

"All right. So back to the subject. You'll take the position?"

"I don't know."

"If you're reluctant because of the money, I can push for an increase in the completion bonus on the contract."

Normally the money would have been a large percentage of her decision. But given the recent change in her financial circumstances, Uncle Camden had made sure that she wouldn't have to worry about it at all.

"It's not the money."

Kenneth took a drink of his soda, and then sat back in his seat. His piercing gaze almost pinned her to the chair. "Is it me, Sasha?" he asked softly. "Be honest. Are you still angry with the way things turned out?"

"No. This has nothing to do with out break-up. I just don't like working with people."

"Ahh, I remember you were kind of into having a lot of personal space."

"I haven't changed that much."

"It's okay though. There's only a small group working on the project. You'll meet a couple of times a week. The rest can be done via email and phone. You'll spend a majority of the time on-site helping with the habitat setup."

"I'll think about it," she started.

He reached across the table and grabbed her hand. "Say yes, Sasha. Don't think about what this could mean to the zoo in terms of donations and visitor rates—think of the animals that you'll save from extinction and the future generations that will be able to know these creatures."

Later she would have to say she'd had a moment of insanity or extreme weakness, but Sasha smiled. "Okay, I'm in."

Kenneth stood up, leaned over the table, and kissed her full on the lips. Shock at his actions froze her in place.

She looked over her shoulder and straight into Arabella's glaring eyes. Before she could warn Kenneth, the woman turned on her heels and disappeared. Life just kept getting interesting.

Chapter 11

When Sasha woke on Saturday morning, she walked over to the window and looked out. A clear sky and bright autumn sun were the perfect invitations to a brisk walk and she needed to get outside. After taking a shower, she went to the closet and grabbed her jacket, jogging pants, sweatshirt, tennis shoes and a pair of gloves.

It was only once she'd gotten to the door and looked down to see Darwin dragging his leash that she stopped to think about something other than getting away from her demons. She opened the door and stared out past the nice fence to see the perfect street and cement sidewalk that led past row after row of million-dollar homes. A sense of claustrophobia was so profound she instinctually backed up and slammed the door. The sound seemed to echo off the walls and highlight just how big and empty the house was. Sasha bent down and fastened the leash on to Darwin's collar. The rapid swishing of his tail made her smile.

"You want to get out just as badly as I do, don't you, boy? Why don't we go to the park?"

While driving toward town, Sasha's stomach growled. Doing something that she'd probably regret later, she pulled into a Starbucks and rolled down the window. Darwin stuck his head out and stared at the outside speaker with a quizzical glance as Sasha perused the menu. "Now only if they had a drive-through sushi spot, all would be perfect, wouldn't it?

The dog pulled his head in and turned around to get off her lap, then lay down in the passenger-side seat. "You agree, too, huh?"

It took her five minutes to decide to fill up on a caramel-laced coffee and thousand-calorie chocolate chip muffin. She gobbled down the muffin in the car. She had to circle the park twice before finding a parking spot. It was Saturday morning and the popular midtown park was filled with people walking dogs and kids, bicycling and jogging.

They were in the last days of autumn. Leaves were on the ground, brown, yellow and red. She drew in the cool crisp air and smiled. Once she'd locked the car and put her keys in her purse, she began to walk with

Darwin trotting alongside. With her coffee in one hand and his leash in the other. She waited until they reached the center of a grassy meadow before putting everything on the ground and releasing Darwin from his leash.

The Jack Russell terrier ran all out toward the nearest tree and after taking a moment to sniff, lifted up his leg and engaged in normal canine behavior. She laughed at the sight as he came running back to her and picked up his ball. In only three weeks since her arrival he'd put on a pound and was back to normal, just as Trey promised. Sasha drew out the ball and before she could release it, Darwin took off like a bullet.

Her thoughts turned back to Trey. She'd promised to call him with an answer as to whether or not she'd be joining the team on constructing the new primate habitat. Since she'd already given her answer to Kenneth the other day, she hadn't rushed to pick up the phone. Part of her was still fuming about his kiss. She'd seen jealousy in the world of nature many times, but Trey needed to know that just because his kisses curled her toes it didn't mean he could dictate her life. Pushing those thoughts aside, Sasha focused on her upcoming tasks.

The project would be unlike anything she'd ever worked on. She'd read studies, visited various zoos and compared notes with the zookeepers. Sasha took another sip of her coffee and breathed. Once more, she was aware of how much her life had changed since

learning of her uncle's death. She'd already made up
her mind to donate money to the zoo. Writing a check
was easy; working to create a replica of the Brazilian
rainforest in the middle of Atlanta would be a definite
challenge.

Sasha threw Darwin's ball for a fifth time. Wagging
his tail, he raced away, jumped, caught it in midair and
then trotted back toward her. She repeated the gesture
over a dozen times and once her arm began to feel the
strain she bent down to pat him on the head.

"Good boy," she praised. "One last time and then we
go for a walk." She stood up and came up against something solid and unmovable.

She glanced over her shoulder, past a hunter green
jacket to Trey's dimple and upturned lips. She meant
to step forward, but almost stepped on Darwin and
moving back she lost her balance and fell against his
chest. His hands grabbed her arms, locking her into
place. For an instant, she wanted to struggle, but her
body did otherwise. Instead, she stayed nestled in his
embrace, feeling the warmth of his body along her
spine as the spice of his cologne heated her senses.

"What are you doing here?"

He leaned forward a little. His breath along her
throat as they were cheek to cheek.

"Rescuing you from the evil tangled leash."

"Get him, Darwin," she urged the dog.

"Siccing the dog on me Sasha—not nice."

"He doesn't bite, Trey."

His hands moved to her stomach, his thumb absent-mindedly stroking. Sasha's shiver had nothing to do with the forty-degree weather. She almost felt like breaking a sweat because she was hotter than she'd ever been. Not even during a two-week stint in the Australian Outback. She turned around still in his arms. His hands moved up her arms, and put her bangs behind her ears. His fingertips brushed against her neck, causing Sasha to inhale softly. As every muscle in her body clenched, she asked, "What are you doing, Trey?"

"Showing Darwin that I'm not a threat to his owner."

"I'm sure he knows that by now."

"You can never be too careful. Dogs can be very territorial."

Sasha's gaze narrowed. "It's not only the canine species that exhibits that behavior. It's a male instinct."

"Exactly."

Sasha glanced around the park, but it didn't seem like any of the guys were paying attention. Then again, she noted that a high percentage of the men were with other men. "I don't think that I'm in any danger. So what are you doing here?"

"Just taking a quick jog before heading into the office."

"It's Saturday."

"Yep, and that's when most of our emergencies come in. Working owners can't bring them in during the week, so they come on their day off."

From the feel of his muscled arms and flat chest,

Sasha could feel the benefits of the time Trey spent keeping in shape. "I would have pegged you for a gym rat."

"Nope. Then again, I never saw you as a Starbucks kind of girl."

"This is a rare indulgence. I'm seldom in areas that have American coffee shops."

Troy leaned down and patted Darwin on the head. "You know Darwin is very well behaved."

"Why do you say that?"

"That German shepherd is the third large dog that's passed in our vicinity."

"And?"

"Small dogs usually bark like crazy when they see big dogs. It's that I'll-get-you-before-you-can-get-me syndrome."

"Ahh, a mixture of Napoleon and Hitler complexes. I'm sure Uncle Camden had Darwin enrolled in canine academy at a young age."

"No matter. So when were you planning on telling me the good news?"

"What news?"

"Kenneth couldn't wait to brag to the director that he sweet-talked you into working on the tamarin exhibit."

Sasha let out an exasperated breath. "I should have known."

"You know I could be upset that he took the credit, but I'm just happy that we'll get to see each sometimes during the day." He paused, and then lowered his voice. "And at evenings."

The nervous butterflies that had started in her stomach moved to her chest as Sasha gazed into his twinkling brown eyes. "Stop flirting with me, Trey."

"Get used to it. I've just started."

"That's the problem. You don't seem to finish what you start."

He ran a hand over her arm, neck, cradled her cheek. "I've always finished what I start. It's just with you I plan to go real slow."

She shook her head. "Not if the end of the line equals commitment. And I've made no secret of my wishes. I want a committed relationship and that's not something you can give me."

"What? I've changed."

"Since when?"

"Since I met you."

As his attention seemed to shift, her eyes narrowed. Like a movie scene, she watched as his eyes left her face. She turned to check out what he was looking at. A tanning-bed, bottle blonde with D cups, tight sports bra and spandex was jogging along the path. Other men's heads turned, as well.

Sasha bent down and furiously gathered her things. She clipped Darwin's leash on and began to walk away. She barked, "Goodbye, Trey."

"Look, why don't we talk about this over breakfast?"

"I'm not hungry."

"Coffee?"

Uncaring of the empty paper cup in her hand, she lied. "I'm giving it up."

"Tea?"

She looked over her shoulder. "Makes me tired."

"How about we head over to the pet store? Grab a fresh dog treat for Darwin."

"He's on a diet."

He jogged after her. "Come on. Give me a chance to explain."

"Bye, Trey," she yelled over her shoulder and broke in to a slow run.

"What now?" he yelled.

Sasha sucked air through her teeth and stomped back toward the parking lot. It was the wind that made her eyes smart, not the stab of self-pity as her eyes glanced down at her own girl-next-door B cups. Then she looked over at Darwin. Thanks to the medication, he was back to his normal self and he was equally curious about male or female, animal or human. "Too bad all males can't be neutered," she growled.

Chapter 12

With one hand on the steering wheel and the other impatiently tapping the gearshift, Trey inched closer to his destination. The Platinum Club, downtown Atlanta's newest and most popular strip club, was packed. *Bachelor party.* He shook his head and wondered what had possessed him to agree to come to Steve's big night. Party was a gross misnomer. It was more like a death row inmate's last meal. A last stand; the last time his friend would be able to hang out with the boys with without checking in with his wife.

After tonight, the banking executive wouldn't be able to look at another woman for the rest of his life.

Trey shook his head. He was glad the man was

getting married in Hawaii *sans* friends and family. Trey never liked weddings. In his life he'd been a flower boy, errand boy, ring bearer and groomsman. He'd sworn after the last all-weekend event that he wouldn't set foot in a church for a wedding unless his little sister or female cousins were walking down the aisle. And the only reason he'd show up in his tuxedo was to make damn sure that the brother who was lucky enough to marry a Blackfox sister realized how hellish his life could become if he messed up.

When he was finally able to get his car valet parked, Trey pulled a ten-dollar bill out of his pocket.

"Park it out front and keep an eye on my car. I'll introduce you to Hamilton's twin when I leave," he said, handing the young man both his keys and the money.

"Yes, sir," the attendant said and eagerly took the keys and the cash.

Trey stepped out of the car and onto the sidewalk. He watched as the valet drove his SUV into one of the only two remaining spaces in the closet parking lot. Just last week he'd taken a day off to have a tracking device installed in his vehicle.

He shoved his hands into his leather coat pockets while trying to summon some enthusiasm for the party. Instead, his thoughts turned in the direction of one person he'd vowed not to think about—Sasha. Trey rubbed his chin as a grin sprang to his lips. Damn, the woman could kiss. Her mouth made him hotter than an August afternoon on the topless French Riviera beach.

He'd been kissing since the fourth grade and if he really thought hard he'd probably be able to recall the girl's name, but nothing could compare to the thrill that shot through his body when the tip of Sasha's tongue flicked across the roof of his mouth.

He entered the club and after telling the concierge that he was here for Steve's bachelor party, Trey was escorted down a winding hallway and found himself on the main floor of the club. Trey wasn't sure how or why but he kept his eyes trained on the back of the hostess's neck and thus avoided the temptation to glance at the dancers on the stage. Even so, his eye encountered dancers dressed in a wide variety of risqué lingerie, stiletto heels, skimpy bikinis, school girl skirts, tiny cut-off tees, thigh-high boots and more.

He let out a sigh of relief as they entered into what he guessed was the VIP room. While separate from the main seating section, the space provided an excellent vantage point of the entire club. He took a seat in a black booth separate from the main seating. The table was filled to capacity with a spread catered for men: buffalo wings, cheese sticks, pizza, salsa and chips, calamari, potato skins and more. Yep, everything a man could want.

"Trey, glad you made it," Jared called out. "Have a seat. You pretty much know the rest of the gang."

He nodded to the other brothers in the midst of eating or drinking. "Wouldn't have missed it for the world. Where's the guest of honor?"

Jared laughed before pointing toward a thirty-foot secondary stage. "He told us he was going to the bathroom, but we all think that he's on the phone with the future wife. Order a drink and sit back. If everything's going to plan, the Steve's-last-night-out show will be on in thirty minutes."

"What?" Trey practically shouted over the thumping bass music.

"I pulled some strings and donated a nice tip to get Steve a starring role in Platinum's soon-to-be-released DVD *Brothers in Bondage*."

Trey hooted with laughter. "You're joking right?"

Jared shook his head and grinned, a sight of pure glee that mixed with the howls of laughter coming from the rest of the bachelor party participants. "No, man. He thinks he's getting an extra special dance."

Sure enough, Steve, the husband-to-be returned with cell phone in hand. It was fifteen minutes, two beers and thoughts about how his mother would kick his butt down the driveway and back if she discovered the combination of money spent and women's clothing taken off at their table that Trey recovered his senses. With all the seductive music and seminaked women from the tiny and petite, to lanky and statuesque, all natural to all implants, all of them came up short in Trey's mind. Feeling relaxed with the slight buzz from the beer, Trey sat back in the booth with his eyes lowered. He would have given the clothes off his back to see Sasha Clayton standing in his bedroom dressing in black lingerie.

Steve's friends kept coming and so did the drinks.

At the same moment Jared looked at his wristwatch, the light dimmed and the spotlights came up on the main stage. "All right, guys. Here's the main attraction we all paid to see."

Trey watched as the Steve was led onstage and tied to a pole by four scantily clad women. The uptight executive looked as though he wanted to pull his way loose and run out the room. During the first song, the women danced while stripping his clothes.

The second song started with the girls stripping him to his underwear. At this point, the girls then begin beating him with his own belt. Then they tied the belt around his neck, and started walking him around the stage like a dog. Steve didn't look like he was having fun, but Trey was.

At that point, the cartoon angel on Trey's right shoulder choked on his own spit and the devil on his left shoulder stabbed him through the chest with his pitchfork. He reached for a barbecue wing and sat back, and began to thoroughly enjoy himself.

"Trey."

Someone kept calling his name. He opened his eyes and a murky fog seemed to hover on the edge of his vision. Trey turned his head to the left and realized that he was in his bed. He closed his eyes at a stabbing pain in the back of his skull and tried to remember what had happened. He'd been waiting on his car, watching two guys arguing about their cars, and he'd been thinking about the color of Sasha's underwear, and that he wanted to invite her to dinner at his place and—

"Trey?" Caleb, his older brother said, leaning over him. "Bro, can you hear me?"

"Stop shouting," he groaned and rolled over.

"How many fingers am I holding up?"

He narrowed his eyes and watched as the finger multiplied, divided and quadrupled before coming into focus. Trey blinked, then answered, "Three."

"Good." He turned to the nightstand and picked up a white bottle. "I stopped by the hospital before picking you up and got a prescription in case you have headaches. How's your head?"

His head felt like a cracked coconut. "Hurts like hell."

Caleb opened the bottle and pulled out two pills. "You want to take these lying down?"

"Not possible. Give me a hand?"

His brother leaned and slowly helped Trey sit up in the bed. He pushed up against the headboard and when he was finally in an upright sitting position, he let his head hang down in the hope that it would help soften the lightening strikes raining down on his skull or quell the bile in his throat.

Trey swallowed a couple of times. "Thanks. You can go and let me die in peace."

"Here," Caleb said, and then placed two of the pills in Trey's hand and gave him a glass of water.

Trey took the pills and gulped down the water. As soon as he was sure that they'd made the one-way journey to his empty stomach, he laid back down. "Was I in a car accident?"

"No, you've got a slight concussion."

"How'd I get that?"

"What's the last thing you remember?"

"I went to Steve's bachelor party at an upscale strip club named Platinum. I had a couple of beers, ate some food, watched strippers tie the groom to a fireman's pole and strip him down to his flannel boxers. Steve passed out before the party ended and I helped Jared take him to his car." He frowned. "Then I handed the valet my ticket."

"That's it?"

He could have added that he clearly remembered standing there imagining Sasha Clayton in a high school cheerleader's uniform, but he held his tongue. "That's it."

"Well, let me fill you in on the missing pieces of your exciting evening. Apparently there was a fight brewing in the parking lot and you decided to play the Good Samaritan and stepped in between two drunk strip club patrons feuding over who dented the other's car. Somebody started throwing punches and by the time the police arrived, you'd managed to get yourself hit upside the head. The police took you downtown and I drove down to bail you out."

Trey felt the pills kick in as the pain receded against

a wave of sleepiness. "How did you know I was in jail?"

"You called me."

"Oh." Trey focused on Caleb's grin. "I did?"

"Yep, I still have the message on my phone. You sounded like a freshman at a busted fraternity party."

His brother mimicked his voice. "*Caleb, I'm going to jail and I need you to get me out. Don't let Mom know.* Damn right, I'm not going to let Mom know. She'd flip if she knew you'd been arrested at a strip club. You had just better pray that the press doesn't get hold of this. The last thing we need is a scandal right before Grandfather's birthday."

Trey winced as the jackhammer against his skull started again. "Sorry."

Caleb shook his head. "You better pray."

"I will when I wake up. You sticking around? I'll be up in a couple of hours."

Caleb shook his head. "Can't. I've got the early shift in the ER tomorrow so I've got to head back. You've got plenty of pain medication. Just follow the instructions and try not to overdose. Get some rest and call me later."

"Thanks again, bro," Trey said sleepily. "I owe you."

"Nah, that's what older brothers are for."

"You didn't tell Marius, did you?" he asked, half-asleep as Caleb prepared to leave the room.

"Yep."

Trey closed his eyes and cursed under his breath. His eldest brother would never let him live this down. If he'd been arrested for fighting, that would be okay. But being at a strip club would guarantee that he'd be the target of Marius jokes for the rest of his life.

"I'll let myself out."

The sound of Caleb's chuckles followed him into sleep.

Chapter 13

Sasha had more than her share of misgivings today. Earlier that morning when she'd pulled into the zoo parking lot, she'd entertained canceling her appointment. Everything in her life had changed and it felt as if by accepting this newest task, she would be accepting that the end of the life that she'd once had. She'd spent her childhood and most of her adult life studying animals in their native habitat. Now she was being asked to use her knowledge to recreate Mother Nature in the middle of a metropolis.

Yet, the second Sasha walked into the project room, she could tell that the team was serious about building a nativelike environment for the Golden Lion tamarins.

The room was filled with research and material as photographs lined the walls, drawings sat in piles on the tables, plants sat scattered on the windowsill. Sasha stared at a lifelike replica of the squirrel-size monkey with long, silky reddish-brown fur. A lionlike mane framed a bare face with pinky purple skin. While in captivity its large round eyes and a snub nose would guarantee its popularity with the zoo's human patrons. Sasha understood that the monkey's features enabled it to find food and avoid predators.

Sasha reached down and picked up a newspaper article announcing the upcoming release. Off the left hand side, her eyes focused on a familiar face in the midst of a group photo. Trey Blackfox was in the picture of the zoo staff. Try as she might Sasha couldn't seem to shake off emotions he stirred up. The man's warm demeanor and smooth confidence was like a magnet, pulling her in and not letting go.

"Ms. Clayton?"

Sasha dropped the article and turned around to face a tall redheaded man with a beard. "Yes?"

"Didn't mean to startle you. I'm Dr. Howell, the lead on the project."

She shook his outstretched hand and smiled. "I would never have recognized you from the photo, Doctor."

"Please call me Roger. After my electric razor died on me, I discovered that the tamarins seemed less skittish when I was around." He reached up and tugged on his beard. "Guess I blend in. Anyway, let's not keep the group waiting. We've got a bit of work to do."

After spending three hours with the project team members whose backgrounds covered the entire spectrum of the zoo as well as outside consultants, she could honestly not think of a better way to spend her time. The zoo didn't just intend to research the animals, it also meant to help facilitate the tamarins' return to the Brazilian rainforest. There was a great deal of planning, design, construction and training. Sasha gathered the stack of research material she would go over later that night and started toward the exit. She turned the corner and ran straight into Trey. Struggling to keep the papers from slipping out of her fingers, she welcomed his steadying hands on her shoulders. "Whoa, you all right?"

Sasha managed to get a grip on the paper and push her purse back up on her shoulder. "Thank you. I'm okay."

"Why didn't you tell me you were starting today?" Trey demanded.

Sasha hadn't expected him to welcome her with open arms and a passionate kiss, but she certainly hadn't expected the angry look she saw in his eyes now. "Does it matter?"

"It does when Kenneth leaves a message on my cell phone with the express purpose of rubbing my nose that today was your first day."

"So this is all about your wounded ego?"

"No, I also wanted to be here to introduce you to the team and take you to lunch on your first day."

His admission took all the wind out of her sails. Several heartbeats passed as Sasha did her best to quash the butterflies in her stomach, but they just moved to her chest and she couldn't do anything but smile. "Okay," she said.

His eyes shot upward from the open area of her blouse. "Huh?"

"Lunch?" she prompted.

He nodded twice before taking her arm. "Right. I know just the right place.

Getting started on the wrong foot by having his eyes glued to Sasha's cleavage wasn't how Trey had planned his afternoon. Then again, his near car accident while watching her cross her legs hadn't been planned, either. It was probably a case of low blood sugar after skipping breakfast that morning or the cold weather. At least that's what he told himself as he watched Sasha bite into a garlic breadstick fresh from the oven.

"I think she's in love."

"Who?" Trey almost dropped his forkful of fettuc-cini. He followed her finger toward a little baby in a stroller. He waved at the little girl and chuckled as the she began to wave her tiny hands.

"She kind of looks like my little sister." He grinned.

"I bet you're very good with kids."

"Kids, animals, politicians," Trey said, shrugging.

He put down his fork, and picked up his iced tea. "I bet kids flock to you like bears to honey."

Her laugh was intoxicating, and he swallowed hard at the way her beautiful brown eyes twinkled.

"You're right about the kids latching on to me, but you forgot the part about me turning and running with my tail between my legs."

Trey raised an eyebrow. "I'm in shock. The world-renowned wildlife researcher is afraid of kids?"

She raised a finger to her mouth. "Shh. It's a secret and if you dare tell anyone I'll have to kill you."

"Ouch." He chuckled and clutched at his chest in imagined pain.

She picked up her fork with her graceful fingers and took a bite of the manicotti. "So tell me what you know about Dr. Howell?"

Just like that, she switched the subject and before Trey knew it, they spent the rest of the lunch discussing her impressions of the team. Learning about Trey's schedule and the numerous advances in veterinary medicine. Leaving the restaurant, they shared interesting details about one another's lives: things they liked to do for fun, favorite movies and memorable moments.

"Thank you for lunch."

Trey got out of his SUV, went around the side and opened the passenger-side door. When he took her hand, the scent of her perfume and warmth of her slender hands reminded him yet again as to why he couldn't get her off his mind.

"You're welcome," he replied, reluctant to release Sasha's hand after assisting her from his vehicle. "I just wanted to make sure you had a good first day."

"You've succeeded."

"I'll walk you back in."

She shook her head and took a step away. "I've kept you from your work long enough. I think I can make it past the insect exhibit without hyperventilating."

As if it was the most natural thing in the world, his fingers caressed the curve of her face. "No doubt in my mind that you, Sasha Clayton, are more than a match for our scorpion admirer."

She smiled. "Goodbye."

Trey put his hands in his jacket pocket and watched her stroll away. Maybe it was just wishful thinking on his part but he could have sworn that there was a little extra swish in her walk. He couldn't have removed his eyes from the curve of her legs, even if he'd wanted to. Even after she'd entered the zoo via the employee entrance, he leaned back against his SUV, staring at the closed door. It took him a moment to realize that he was actually cold. Trey rubbed his brow, jumped back in his SUV and turned on the engine. For a moment, he let the engine idle as he struggled with a momentary surge of panic as he tried to recall a time when he'd wanted something as badly as he wanted Sasha. Just as fast as the sensation hit, it disappeared. Trey looked up into the rearview mirror and winked at his reflection. Trey Blackfox had always gotten what he wanted.

Chapter 14

"So this is where you've been hiding."

"Hello, Trey."

He looked around and noticed that the indoor exhibit was empty except for Sasha. "How long have you been here?"

"A few hours, I think. I've lost track of time."

"Where are the others?"

She leaned back on her knees and rounded her shoulders. "Since its Friday, I imagine that most are home with their families or out starting off the weekend with a drink."

"Yet, you're still here." He'd thought about Sasha all day. Hell, he had her on his mind all week. They'd spoken to each other on the phone almost every day, and the midnight softness of her voice had sent him into the bathroom for a quick cold shower three nights in a row.

"As are you."

Her soft smile pulled him from his uncertain thoughts and he went over to where she was kneeling at one of the flowerbeds. She patted the ground next to her and Trey bent down. "I got a call about a llama with a nasty inner ear infection. I called your cell phone and you didn't pick up." Trey reached over and, unasked, began digging a small hole with a garden tool.

"How did you know I was here?"

"I didn't. I always stop by to see how things are going."

"When I was a little girl my mother would plant a garden in the spring even if we were scheduled to leave before being able to pick them. She told me that they would be a gift to the family that came after us. I never realized how rejuvenating planting could be."

He watched, fascinated by her elegant hands, hands that competently set a bunch of new seedlings into their new homes. Never in his life had Trey thought that something so simple could turn him on, but the sight of her glowing eyes and dirt-stained cheek ignited a blaze of lust in the pit of his gut.

Her softly worded question broke his concentration.

"Trey, could you pass me the trowel, please?"

He handed it over and proceeded to pick up another plant and lower it into the freshly dug hole.

"Thank you."

"So are you going to tell me what's got you digging holes at—" Trey paused to look at this watch "—seven o'clock in the evening?"

"I talked to my mother today."

"Is everything alright with your parents?"

"I was going to tell her about the inheritance, but then she told me that Dad was nominated for an award. I didn't have the heart to say anything."

"So you're doing this to keep your mind off the situation?"

She returned the trowel to a small box and pulled off her gloves. "Exactly, and if I go home, the mansion will make me feel even guiltier."

"Well, I know another way to take your mind off the situation," Trey said, following the curve of her neck and wondering if he'd come down with some new form of delirium. Since her arrival in Atlanta, they'd taken long drives, had dinner together at numerous restaurants, shared lunches at the zoo and sat next to one another at various foundation meetings. But, it wasn't enough that he was stopping by the exhibit to see her every day and he sometimes followed her home at night. Truth was, he loved spending time with her, eagerly anticipated leaving the office to fight traffic to catch a glimpse of her at work or getting into her car.

It felt like Christmas morning every time they were alone. He couldn't remember how long it had been since he'd laughed so hard his chest hurt. He loved the soft lilt of her voice and the stories she told of her parents, the adventures they'd had traveling the world and how she was always getting into trouble. He loved the way the corners of her mouth titled upwards in a mischievous smile. He found that he liked that smile on her, even if it had the effect of making him hard.

"I'm not ready to spend the night with you, Trey."

Trey's mouth went dry. "Not yet, huh? Does that mean there's a chance?"

"Stranger things have happened."

He grinned. "When you and I get together, Sasha Clayton, you'll be able to think of many adjectives to describe us, but *strange* won't be one of them."

He helped her stand and even after she'd gotten her balance, he didn't let go of her hands. Instead, he captured her lips with his own and kissed her until they both ran out of air. When he pulled back and looked down into her dark eyes, she had to struggle not to do it again. "I've wanted to do that all day."

Her tongue darted out over her bottom lip. "You must have had a long day."

"Oh, yes. And I'll tell you all about it over dinner."

"Are you inviting me out to dinner?"

"No, I'm inviting you to my home for dinner."

Her smile lit up her face. "I might have plans."

"Trust me. The plants aren't going anywhere and neither is this zoo. But you and I are going to head to my place for the best chicken you've had in your life."

"That's a big boast."

"It'll be so good that you'll want to kick yourself because you won't be able to finish it."

Sasha laughed. "Not in this lifetime. My parents never had to threaten to send my food to the starving children in Africa, because I learned early on to clean my plate."

He laughed at the saucy way her head bobbed from side to side. "All right, then. Let's get out of here."

Sasha had to admit Trey hadn't lied about his culinary skills. The stuffed chicken was sweet and tangy, the white meat so juicy she was almost tempted to go back for seconds. While she'd set the table, he'd whipped up a spinach salad, taken the garlic bread out of the oven and poured two glasses of wine. Dinner had been complete with slow jazz on the stereo and a glass-encased candle on the table.

"So where'd you learn how to cook like that?" Sasha asked after they'd cleared the table and placed the last plate into the dishwasher. If she hadn't been in the loft while he'd prepared the meal, she would have checked the garbage for gourmet take-out boxes.

"My mom was a very forward-thinking Southern woman. She and Dad met at Howard," he said.

She pulled up one of the barstools next to the breakfast bar and watched as Trey operated the espresso maker. He placed two coffee-filled mugs, sugar and cream on a wooden serving tray.

He continued, "They met at a party late one Sunday

night when all the restaurants were closed and the stores were closed for the day. My dad was starving because he didn't know how to cook and didn't have any food back at his apartment. Mom took pity on the poor man and took him home to her parents."

Sasha followed Trey into the living room and watched as he placed the tray on a side bar next to a small round table that held an antique-looking chess set.

"Here you go."

Sasha took the cup from Trey's outstretched hand and gave him a warm smile. The first sip of the warm chocolate-laced coffee made her lips inch higher. She picked up her cup of coffee as Trey gestured for her to take a seat in the comfortable leather chair. "Don't stop there—you've got to finish the story," she urged.

Trey took a seat in the opposite chair. "Well, Dad always told me that he fell in love with my mother when she invited him over to dinner, but couldn't really talk to her with her parents glaring at him from the other end of the table. So he decided that he'd learn how to cook so he could impress her."

He put down his cup and leaned forward. "How about a game of chess?" he asked.

She leaned forward, eager to hear the rest of the story. "Trey. The story. You have to finish the story first."

"Where was I? Oh, Dad decided that he'd learn how to cook. So he invited my mom over for dinner one

Sunday afternoon. He wanted to make her some fried chicken, but ended up setting fire to the kitchen. My mom, being the smart woman she was, had come prepared. They ended up eating cold ham sandwiches."

"So how does this story relate to the wonderful gourmet dinner you just whipped up?"

"Mom didn't want some crafty upper-class girl enticing me back to her apartment with promises of home-cooked meals."

"So she taught you how to cook?" Sasha guessed.

Trey nodded and set down his mug. "She made all of us peel potatoes, chop onions and skin catfish. Mom taught the basics and from there I learned to improvise."

He was probably very good at improvising, she thought, her stomach fluttering a little. Why on earth was she getting turned on by that statement? The answer was way too easy. Everything about him was sexy, from his muscled physique to the baritone of his voice and hypnotic brown eyes.

"How about some mental stimulation?"

"Hmm. I'm game."

"Good. Chess."

"What's the stakes?" Sasha never played any game unless she had something to lose. Which made the game all the more interesting and winning all the more sweet.

"If I win, you spend the night."

Spend the night. The temperature in the loft seemed

to rocket up ten degrees. His voice was smooth like silk brushing against her skin. The phrase did a triple loop in her head. It sounded as innocent as a slumber party, but the last thing she imagined was sleeping. Her pelvic muscles clenched as images of his lips on sensitive areas of her skin flashed through her mind. Lord, spending the night with Trey was a bad idea. So bad that it was good. With all the sexual tension that had been building since the day they first met, sex with him would be better than good—it would be phenomenal. Better than chocolate.

Sasha hesitated, not because she wasn't confident, but even professional players lost pieces. Moreover, she wasn't so sure that she wanted Trey to see just how color-coordinated and sheer her lingerie was.

"Afraid?"

"No," she responded, taking a breath and faking a sense of bravado. "And if I win?"

He spread his arms wide. "Name it and you can claim it."

"That's pretty magnanimous of you."

"I don't intend to lose, Sasha."

Grinning, he took off his watch, then proceeded to remove his cufflinks. "Now for the new rules."

Sasha narrowed her eyes. She really hadn't even accepted the wager yet. "Rules?"

"For every piece you win, the opponent loses a piece of clothing. Not including jewelry."

She gave him an annoyed glance. "No fair. You've

been playing this since puberty and it only adds to your possible prize."

"I'm just upping the stakes. I can understand if you're nervous." He reached over and removed two pieces from the board. "So I'll start out with a handicap."

The mood between them during dinner had been easy and relaxed, but now the sexual tension permeated the air. Ten minutes into the game, she lost her shoes and her socks. During winter when Sasha was growing up, she'd hated it when her mother wouldn't let her leave the house without at least two layers of clothing. Now she would have given anything to have her pink long johns, cotton turtleneck and sweater.

She stared at the board, very aware that Trey's intense eyes watched her. "I think you should take another handicap."

"I think you should take off your blouse and that will be all the handicap you need."

Sasha fell silent as her body warmed at the huskiness in his voice. "Wouldn't that defeat the purpose of the game?" she asked, and realized that she knew the answer.

"No, but it might hasten my victory."

Trey's hand reached over the table and cupped her face. Forced into eye contact, her stomach fluttered. "I don't intend to lose, Trey."

"And I can't let you win, Sasha."

On her next move, Sasha captured his only knight

and instead of taking off his socks, Trey unbuttoned his shirt and shrugged it off. Her mouth went dry and what little chess strategy she remembered vanished at the sight of his bare chest.

No man should be that smooth and sexy.

Although Sasha had eaten a mere hour before, she was ravenous with another kind of hunger. She dragged her eyes away and stared blindly at the board until her senses returned and when they did, she frowned. Something was odd.

Trey cleared his throat and grinned at the top of Sasha's head. He dangled her pawn in front of her eyes. "Missing something?"

"You took off your shirt on purpose," she said.

It took a lot of effort, but he managed to keep from laughing at the look of betrayal on Sasha's face. "Off."

She stood, unzipped her slacks, slid them off, then stepped out. The rush of cold air combined with the heat of Trey's stare sent tingles all over her body. She sat down and they resumed the game with an even greater intensity. It took only a few more moves before he took her knight, and then she took his bishop.

A few minutes later, Trey growled, "Check."

Sasha sat clothed solely in the underwear she hadn't wanted Trey to see as he sat back naked but for boxer shorts. His eyes deliberately moved from her face to her breasts.

"Stand up and take it off," he said, his voice husky and deep.

God, she needed air. Sasha had never been so hot in her life. It had been a long time since she'd undressed in front of a man. An eternity since her blood thrummed with desire. She knew that she should stay seated and try to figure out how to give up without losing, but she was enjoying this way too much.

She stood facing Trey but with her face turned away. Her fingers trembled so much it took her three tries to undue the clasp. But she couldn't bring herself to remove the sheer fabric.

Trey stood and walked around to the back of her chair. "Relax, Sasha," he purred in her ear. "I'm only going to do what you want me to do."

Sasha swallowed as she felt his hard body pressed against her backside. There was something wonderfully erotic about his embrace. She stared straight ahead into the darkened window and she could see the silhouette of their reflection. He ran his fingers through her hair a moment before his mouth suckled on the curve of her neck. Sasha trembled as the unexpected pleasure rushed through her. Trey intensified his assault, dragging his teeth over her skin, gently nipping her skin. Her eyes fluttered closed and she moaned.

His mouth moved to her ear and he traced the outline with his tongue before asking in a husky voice, "Liked that, didn't you?"

Sasha couldn't have answered to save her life.

He hooked his thumbs under her bra and slid it off until Sasha raised her hands to capture it. He began to tease her ear with his tongue. Sasha dropped her arms and arched back against him, automatically responding to his touch as chills swept over her skin. His lips caressed her neck as he moved his upward to cup her breasts while he slowly pressed himself against her.

Sasha groaned in pleasure as his hands toyed with her body. His left hand massaged her left nipple while he slid the other down her body. His fingertips trailed over her skin and paused at the band of her panties.

"Do you want me to touch you here?" he asked. He slowly slid his hand underneath her satin panties and dipped two of his fingers against her soft, wet heat.

Her arms clung to his shoulders, almost whimpering with need. "Please."

Almost to his breaking point, Trey turned Sasha around. Immediately his mouth captured hers, sucking her tongue into his mouth, possessing it at the same time his hands caressed her arch of her spine. Dangerously close to losing his self-control and taking her on the sofa, Trey pulled back and trailed kisses down her neck before saying in a husky voice, "We can sit down and continue our game or we can go upstairs. I need you to tell me what you want." He breathed into her ear.

Sasha licked her lips and struggled to breathe as Trey continued to tease her mercilessly. Her fingers locked on to his hips and she rubbed herself against him as his hand swept downward to run against her inner thigh. Her body would willingly give him anything he wanted just to soothe the aching between the apex of her thighs. She moaned, unable to tell him anything but the truth. "I want you."

Releasing a ragged breath of relief, Trey pressed his erection against her buttocks. During the entire chess match, he'd pictured Sasha writhing underneath him in his bed. With every move he'd made on the chess board, he'd suckled her breasts, caressed her flesh or kissed her lips. Now, he would repeat everything but this time for real. Gently, he took Sasha's hand and led her upstairs to his bedroom.

Without turning on the light, he led her over to the side of the bed, and made short work of removing the final barriers between them. The second her panties hit the floor, she pushed the duvet covers back and prepared to get into bed.

Trey grabbed Sasha from behind and the sensation of skin-to-skin contact was so exquisite, it wrung a groan from his lips. "Not yet." He wanted her ready. Hell, he wanted her more than ready. It might give him a heart attack but Trey was determined to give Sasha more pleasure than she could stand.

She turned around in Trey's arms and stepped closer to his body. "You aren't changing your mind are you, Doctor?"

"Not possible."

"Then take me to bed," she growled impatiently before crawling into his bed on her hands and knees. Even in the dim glow from the city lights, he could see the heated look in Sasha's eyes. Trey's entire body went still and it wasn't until after releasing a ragged breath that his brain kicked back in. Quickly opening the nightstand drawer, he pulled out a condom and sheathed himself.

Trey joined her on the bed, positioned himself behind her, and slid one hand from the back of her neck down her spine, across her bare behind and between her thighs. Sasha arched her back and moaned. He pulled his fingers back, positioned his throbbing shaft and moved into her.

Sasha cried out and Trey froze when he heard her cry of pain. He began to pull out, but she tightened her legs together. He leaned forward, his body covering hers, wrapped his right arm around her waist and supported himself on his left elbow and forearm. "I don't want to hurt you, Sasha," he breathed heavily into her ear.

She shook her head from side to side. "Make love to me, Trey," she moaned, losing herself to the sensation of him thick inside her. "You won't hurt me."

He started slowly, moving his hips in a smooth rhythm and gradually began to increase the pace, giving her more, touching just the right spot deep inside her. Each stroke brought her closer to orgasm. Pleasure of an intensity that she'd never experienced before started deep inside and cascaded outward with each stroke. And, when she felt his mouth on her shoulder and the hard edges of his teeth on her skin, it rippled over her skin, and flooded every sense from head to toe. When completion came, Sasha's entire body convulsed, and she fell forward onto the bed.

Trey growled deep in this throat as he exploded inside her. He wanted to stay just where he was and savor every moment. Their bodies still joined together, he leaned to the side and used his left arm to pull the covers over them both. A few heartbeats later, Trey smiled at Sasha's soft little snore. Trey hugged her to him and held, simply enjoying the sensation of stroking her bare stomach.

Minutes passed and all he did was lie there behind her and just watched her. Fierce protectiveness flooded him as some new part wanted to brand her as his own. Closing his eyes, he buried his face in her hair, inhaled the sweet fragrance and slept.

An hour later, Trey opened his eyes to see Sasha smiling at him. "Have a nice nap?" He grinned.

"Best sleep I've had in months."

"Good, now how about I run out to the video store and we spend the day naked in bed watching old movies?"

"So you're just going to play hooky at the clinic?"

"That's what I have partners and assistants for. They can pick up the slack for a day or two."

"I'm tempted, but…"

He reached over and playfully nipped her shoulder. "But what? You don't have to punch the clock—you're rich."

Sasha winced as though he'd said some dirty word. "I'm not rich. My pets are," she argued.

Trey laughed. A sound that came from his soul. Everything about her fascinated him. This was over the top after spending half his life being chased by women who viewed his money and connections as a pot of gold at the end of a rainbow; he'd met that one girl he'd didn't think existed. Sasha actually had a major hang-up about having money.

This is the one, a voice seemed to whisper at the back of his mind but he shut it out and concentrated on the swell of her breast peeking out over the top of the duvet.

"Why are you thinking about tomorrow when tonight hasn't ended? It's an hour until midnight. And there's a lot that can happen in an hour," Sasha murmured, tickling his skin.

"So what happens at midnight, sweetness? Do you turn into a werewolf?" he asked, nuzzling the curve of her neck. Trey inhaled deeply, loving her scent, loving every second they spent together. Reaching over he wrapped his arm around her stomach and pulled her tight against him.

She chuckled softly and then swiftly inhaled as his fingers moved south. "Wrong fairy tale. This heroine disappears at midnight."

Trey lowered his head and used his tongue to make slow circles over her nipples. "How about you stay for breakfast?"

"I have a meeting with the new foundation president in the morning."

His hand moved between her thighs and his finger slid into her. "I'll make sure you get home early."

Their gazes locked, and Trey knew then that he would never get enough of seeing her heavily lidded gaze, hearing her small moans or feeling the way her body reacted to his touch.

Sasha's tongue darted out and he barely resisted the urge to kiss her. "I'm going to sleep in my own bed tonight, Trey," she stated.

His eyes narrowed at the challenge in her tone and he moved his fingers in and out, carefully teasing her sensitive nub, making her squeal with pleasure.

"We'll see," he said aloud before his mouth swept down on hers, cutting off her response. Trey had every intention of keeping Sasha with him all day and all night.

Chapter 15

It was Saturday evening and instead of enjoying her weekend either at home with Jackson and the pets or spending time with Trey, Sasha was yet again participating in a social function. Lord, she hated being in large gatherings and especially loathed being in front of cameras. Flashbulbs blinded her as the president of the Atlanta zoo took his seat. Sasha rubbed her eyes to clear the blue shadow left by looking into the flashing lights. She half wished she'd never taken on the project, but the fact that the project would help bring the tamarin population back from the edge of extinction was her only consolation.

She stood with Kenneth on one side and a group of

keepers, staff veterinarians and biologists on the other. She had dressed in a dark green evening dress because she'd wanted to blend into the tropical forest theme. Nevertheless, the majority of the event goers wearing black had negated her efforts. She stood out from the rest of the crowd.

The cameras flashed to life as the zoo's publicist, Amy Reed, switched on the microphones, pointed to the first reporter, and the questions began. Sasha scanned the room until her eyes fell on Trey. He was dressed impeccably in a single-breasted suit, striped shirt and tie. When Trey caught her glance, his mouth eased into a slow smile, and just that look sent a flash of heat throughout her body.

The responsive smile that had readily sprung to her lips fell and her eyes narrowed on the woman close to his side: Arabella Mays. Kenneth had assured her that his current girlfriend was well aware that he and Sasha were *just friends*, but she didn't believe it. There hadn't been a week yet that Arabella hadn't stopped by the exhibit to chat with Sasha and ask intrusive personal questions.

She'd never thought of herself as a jealous woman. But the moment Trey turned his head to speak to Arabella, Sasha wanted to leap off the stage and pull every strand of hair out of the other woman's head.

"Chin up," Kenneth whispered after tapping her shoulder. "It's almost over."

Sasha turned her head to look at him and did her

level best not to glare. The last month and a half couldn't have been more perfect. There had been mornings when she'd woken in her bed or in Trey's and pinched herself. With Trey's help she'd hired the appropriate people to run her godfather's foundation. She'd come to love working at the zoo. Yet, the open gala celebration served as a reminder that her assignment was ending and she would have to re-examine her plans. "If I'd known that I'd have to sit up here, I wouldn't have come."

"That's exactly why I didn't tell you," he replied, a twinkle in his dark eyes.

Sasha gritted her teeth and crossed her legs. "I'm leaving right after this."

"Not possible." Kenneth shook his head. "You're scheduled for a few team pictures. Not to mention there's going to be music and I've got a reservation on your dance card, Sasha Clayton."

He leaned closer to her and under the cover of the table, placed his hand on her thigh and squeezed. Sasha retaliated by moving her heel into his foot.

He jerked his hand away. "Ouch, what did you do that for?"

"For putting me in the middle of your relationship problems with Arabella," she hissed and stepped on his foot again. "That was for hinting to Trey that you wanted to resume our past relationship."

For those in the audience Kenneth's facial expression hadn't changed during the exchange. Sasha, on the other hand, knew better. She could see the ticking in his cheek.

"Trey told you?"

Sasha's eyes narrowed. "He didn't have to. You haven't changed all that much. You've never liked to share anything or anyone."

"Well he obviously didn't get the hint. Now that you've broken my foot, can we call it even?"

She gave him an incredulous look and then sighed deeply. "Not until I get out of here."

"Ms. Clayton, a question?"

Sasha blinked as someone shoved the microphone into her hand. Her throat went dry as she looked up and found herself the focus of the audience's attention. "Yes?"

"Is it true that the exhibit will be named in honor of your late godfather, Camden Ridgestone?"

She swallowed hard, hating the reporter for publicly announcing her relationship to Uncle Camden. "I was unaware of that proposal."

"Now that the exhibit is complete, will you remain at the zoo?"

"I started the project on a volunteer basis. Now that the tamarins are comfortably resettled into their new home, my job is done and I will leave them in the care of Zoo Atlanta's well-qualified staff."

Sasha passed the microphone back to the publicist and sat back with a sigh of relief.

As the question session ended, the zoo's president

took his place at the podium. "The new primate exhibit will feature Golden Tamarin lions in a setting as close to their natural habitat as possible. Thanks to our patrons and generous corporate and private donations, we've been able to ship in native Brazilian vegetation and trees. This will not only enrich the visiting community, but also allow for increased possibility of re-introduction of the monkeys to the wild."

Sasha tensed as the president turned his attention to their group. "I'd also like for you to join me in an extra heartfelt thank you on the behalf of the Atlanta Zoo board to the team that made all this possible."

The president paused as the audience began to applaud. "I don't often go back on my word, but my conscience won't let me leave this podium without expressing my gratitude to a departed friend and zoo advocate, Camden Ridgestone. In his life, he gave of his time and his money. With his passing, he established a five-million-dollar trust fund for our exhibit. Moreover, he's left his legacy in Sasha's capable hands."

Sasha froze as dozens of flashbulbs momentarily blinded her.

"Smile," Kenneth hissed.

She did her best as her vision started to return. The zoo's president returned his attention to the audience and picked up a champagne flute from the podium. "Raise your glasses. We're excited and proud to open this gala on behalf of the new Ridgestone Primate exhibit."

* * *

All it took was the free-flowing alcohol to turn the formal gala into a dance party. An hour after the opening ceremony, Sasha picked up her purse from the back of her chair and started for the nearest exit. She'd spent the past half hour fielding personal questions from the press. As she took a few steps a hand wrapped around her waist.

"Kenneth, I'm not dancing with you," she said.

"That's good to hear, sweetness."

The sound of Trey's voice so close to her ear made her shiver. Dozens of emotions skittered through her mind. Relief. Uncertainty. Irritation. "Trey."

"Good job up there," he said.

She blinked twice and then breathed deeply. A few heartbeats before, her nerves had been on the tips of her fingernails. Now, the simple touch of his hand on her arm, the rich tenor of his voice and the warmth of his regard washed all nervousness away. "Thank you."

"Going somewhere?" He took a step closer and Sasha studied him. Heavens, he looked good enough to eat.

She toyed with her purse. "Anywhere away from all these people."

"Not yet," Trey said. "I think that I've earned at least one celebratory dance."

Before Sasha could voice the protest he saw in her eyes, he took her hand and moved onto the dance floor. Only after he wrapped his arms around her hips and settled her snug against his body did he relax. Even with Arabella's annoying chatter and Kenneth's deliberate baiting, Trey couldn't have kept his eyes off Sasha even if he'd wanted to. Even now, his gaze lingered on the curve of her neck. He itched to kiss her. Even as the tempo of the music increased, he kept a slow rocking motion. He grew hard as her thighs brushed against him.

"I'll make it worth your while if you hum that tune to me tonight."

She pulled back and her lips opened, curved upward. "My mother loves this song. She'd sing it when she was working in the garden."

"I should have guessed," he grinned.

"Guessed what?"

"That you were an old school girl."

"Not true. I'm a jazz girl first," she proclaimed.

"Hmm, I'll have to remember that." He smiled. "I don't know, I always thought of you as the play-it-straight type. You know those jazz lovers get a little wild sometimes," he hinted.

"I've had my fair share of walking on the wild side," she ruefully admitted. "I've got an arrest record in South Africa and a outstanding traffic violation in Sweden."

"I'm shocked." Trey's eyes widened in mock surprise. "Could this be Sasha Clayton admitting to breaking the rules?"

"Only when absolutely necessary. Unlike you," she responded.

"Me?" he echoed trying to pull off a wide-eyed look of innocence.

She pointed a finger at his chest and chuckled. "Yes, you. Mr. U-turn on a one-way street."

"That was an accident."

"Really?" Her eyebrows lifted.

"No," he admitted sheepishly.

"Let's not forget the time you…"

"Okay, woman." Trey moved his lands down and pinched her lightly on the rear. "No need to recount all my sins."

"Oh, I think there's a need," she said huskily. The wicked twinkle in her eyes sent another wave of lust through him. He imagined pulling off her panty hose and removing the sexy underwear he guessed she wore underneath the dress.

"We need to get out of here now," he finished for her. With one hand in his pocket pulling out keys, and the other one in Sasha's hands, Trey took his woman home.

Chapter 16

Saturday morning Trey stood alongside the golf cart with his hands in his coat pocket and watched as his father wiped off the golf club.

"So you drove all the way up here to hang out with your dad, huh?"

"Just thought we could get a little father and son time in before you left on vacation." He reached over and patted his father's shoulder. "Nothing wrong with that, is there?

"Nothing at all. Just surprised. Your mother tells me you're living quite the life down there in Atlanta."

He shrugged. "You know how women are. They get hold of something and blow it out of proportion."

"Maybe some women. Definitely your aunt Mary and Nettie, but your mother has an uncanny habit of calling a spade a spade."

Trey hated to admit it, but his father was right. Moreover, his mother had never been far off with her observations on life. She had one-hundred-percent accuracy when it came to the members of their family.

Not long ago, Trey remembered that he had had everything he'd ever wanted. Today, not much had changed in his life. Unless he factored in Sasha.

They'd only known each other for a few months, but he felt like she'd always been with him. Although she'd only left for New York the night before, he also missed her like crazy.

"You plan on sitting this one out, son?"

Trey pushed Sasha's image from his mind and concentrated on their golf game. He stepped up to the tee and focused on the faraway white flag. He swung and watched helplessly as his ball landed in a side pocket of sand.

"Not bad." His dad clapped a hand on his shoulder, and chuckled. "Not good, either."

"Too windy," Trey explained lamely.

"You mean too lazy. I bet you haven't been on a course since we held that company event last year."

"No time. I spend a lot of my Saturdays at the clinic."

"You need to make time to relax, son. Look at me. It's Saturday and you're not in the office. I never thought I'd see the day."

"I'm not needed. I'll dress up and make a nice

speech or two at the board meetings, but I have to hand it to Marius, he's stepped up to the plate and knocked one out of the park."

They put away their clubs and settled into the golf cart. Trey looked to the left and smiled. His father loved driving. Didn't matter if the thing had two wheels or eighteen. Something about the road or the steering wheel had always drawn his father. Heck, it drove his whole family. His grandfather had started the trucking business because of his love of the road. Every one of his siblings and cousins had known the basics of driving a car before learning how to ride a bike.

"Yeah, thanks to Marcus's success with the company, I can fund the clinic while barely putting a dent in my trust fund."

"It's going to be tax time soon and your mother and I will need all the deductions we can get. Why don't you give a call to Tom and have him write out a check to that foundation of yours."

"I've never been one to turn down a helping hand. I'll give him a call on Monday."

His father came to a stop behind another group of golfers and Trey leaned back, enjoying the warmth of the sun. A few moments passed in silence before his father spoke. "So are you going to come to Grandfather's birthday party?"

"Of course," Trey answered.

"You won't be bringing one of those dime-a-dozen girls with air between their ears as your date, will you?"

Trey should have known that was coming. Predicted it like traffic on a football Sunday when the Falcons played in the Georgia dome. Yet he'd still hoped to avoid talking with his father about women. Samuel Blackfox considered himself an expert on women because he'd grown up with two sisters, was still married to his high school sweetheart and raised a daughter.

Trying to evade the question, Trey said, "I'll probably ride up in the new car, and I might bring some flowers for Grandmother. And I have a box of Havana's best cigars for Grandfather."

"Boy, don't try to change the subject. Now just tell me the truth and let's get this out of the way. If she's pregnant you've got to marry the girl."

"What!" Trey's shout earned him a few nasty looks from the other golfers waiting to tee off. "Dad, what are you talking about?"

"Don't fool with me. I heard about you running around with all those women. Your mother told me about her talk with that other veterinarian."

"What is it with you and Mom? Do the two of you not have enough to do or something? I'm not even dating." Technically, he was telling the truth. But at the moment, he was dancing on a thin line. He wasn't dating Sasha. *Dating* was too casual a word for what was going on between them. For the first time in years, he could honestly say he was in a relationship and he wanted to keep that fact a secret for as long as possible.

"You don't have to be dating. Women these days are different. They want what they want and they're not going to wait until a ring to get it. You have to be careful. Getting a girl pregnant is the least of your worries. They've got stuff out there now that will kill you."

Trey waved his hand and wanted to jump out the cart and head back to the clubhouse, but the half mile walk didn't appeal to his already unsettled stomach. His job hadn't given him a day of stress in his life. There was always the challenge of healing an animal who couldn't exactly tell you what was wrong. But the job had never given him indigestion. The hearty breakfast he'd consumed an hour before didn't feel as good as it had before his father started making comments and implying he was the whore of Babylon.

"You've got my word that there won't be an illegitimate Blackfox kid coming from me."

"I'll still feel better if you settle down."

"How much more settled could I be? I'm not ready to get married and even if I were there are a lot of beautiful, intelligent…" He paused, and then added, "Church-going women in Atlanta. It might take me a while and I'm pretty busy with work."

"Well, seeing one woman at a time might help," his father grumbled.

Trey swallowed a sigh of relief as the hole in front of them opened up and they could resume playing. *One woman at a time, huh,* he chuckled. *Looks like I'm ahead of the game this time.*

Chapter 17

Sasha was miserable. Even after spending the day shopping with her best friend and dining at some of New York's trendiest restaurants, she couldn't shake the sense of emptiness that had gripped her the moment Trey had dropped her off at the airport. Now, alone in her Brooklyn apartment, she sat back against the headboard and closed her eyes.

The radiator emitted a low hiss as the steam forced its way out of the small pipe. A light snow continued to fall outside and would coat the city with a layer of ice by the morning. Initially she'd made the impulsive decision to come to New York to see her best friend. After being named Atlanta's newest heiress on the front page of the Metro section of the local newspaper and Trey's erratic behavior, it had been essential that she get away for a little while.

Some days when she was with him, they would talk about the future and jokingly pick the names of their future children. Other days, the mere hint that she wanted to know his thoughts about where their relationship was headed would cause him to change the topic of their conversation.

Opening her eyes, she got out of bed and started toward the closet. She might have looked out the window and watched the snowfall or flipped on the ancient nineteen-inch television she'd purchased while in-between assignments. Instead, she decided to finish boxing her possessions and ship them down south. Regardless of how things turned out with Trey, her life was in Atlanta.

A part of her held on to the certainty that he was "the one." The soul mate who'd been put on earth just for her. The other part waited for the other shoe to drop and refused to believe that something so good could be real. She'd sworn to herself that she would not think of him and that she would be open to meeting other people, but she ended up ignoring all of Lena's male friends and constantly comparing all the guys she met to Trey.

Her cell phone rang just as she placed one of her many textbooks into a box. Her head came up and her heart jumped at the familiar ring. Sasha had owned the phone for weeks and had been unable to do more than turn it on and off. It had taken Trey mere minutes to program the ringer. She smiled at the classical tune. Dropping her books in to the box, she picked up the phone. "Hello."

"Throw any snowballs?"

"Not yet." Sasha pushed her clothing aside and sat down on the love seat. "Maybe in the morning. Did it snow there?"

"Not even a flurry. One of the assistants had to take the day off. Half of the Atlanta school systems decided to close the schools just in case of black ice." His voice melted away her misgivings and warmed her heart.

"How are things at the clinic?"

"Insane. Ever since the zoo opening, it's been non-stop appointments. We're even thinking about hiring two more doctors so I can spend more time at the zoo."

"I'm sorry."

"It's not your fault. If you want to lay blame anywhere it should be at Arabella's door."

Sasha gripped the cell phone tighter and sat up at the mention of the woman's name. "W-what does Arabella have to do with this?"

"She convinced a reporter to do a big spread on the exhibit."

"That witch. I'm going to kill Kenneth when I get back."

"No need. I've got everything taken care of."

"What did you do?"

"All you need to know is that on Sunday morning there's going to be a familiar couple in the engagement announcement section."

"You got Kenneth to propose?" she shrieked. "How in the world did you do that?"

"I introduced him to my friends Grey Goose and Jim Bean."

"Have I met them?"

He chuckled. "Not unless you've been experimenting behind the wet bar. Grey Goose is vodka and Jim Bean is whiskey."

"You got him drunk," she surmised.

"All I had to do was make a few carefully placed suggestions and then I called Arabella to pick him up."

"That was devious and brilliant, Trey. They'll make each other miserable."

"Thank you."

"Remind me never to get on your bad side."

"With you, beautiful, that's not possible. I just wish you were at my side now. The bed misses you."

She shivered. "Only the bed?"

"No, the shower, too. Not to mention the chess set. I'm waiting for a repeat game."

"Trey."

"Yes?"

"I miss you."

Her heart leaped in her throat at the silence. With all of the uncertainty, not knowing if he cared for her, Sasha needed to hear the words.

"I miss you, too."

The tension drained out of her shoulders, leaving her almost boneless.

"Now get some sleep, beautiful, and enjoy the city."

"Good night, Trey."

"Sweet dreams."

The line went dead. Sasha closed the cell phone and plopped back on the sofa. When did telling someone that she missed them get to be so complicated? When did the thought of not looking into Trey's eyes, not feeling his fingertips run lightly over her skin, not hearing his voice husky in her ears, leave Sasha with a knot in her stomach? What had the woman who could go weeks without seeing another human being, turn into the scared girl who could not go a day without a man?

Feeling the beginnings of a headache behind her eyes, she sat up and grabbed a handful of unopened mail. I'm going to have to forward my mail, she thought to herself and flipped through envelope after envelope of credit card offers until she came to a postcard from Barbados. Sasha froze at the sight of her father's nearly illegible writing.

She read the short missive quickly and the pain in her head exploded into pounding as she read the final sentence. *Will return home on the 30th. Talk to you then.* She closed her eyes. She had two weeks until her reprieve ended. A mere fourteen days to figure out a way to tell her father about the inheritance, about her deception and about Trey.

Dropping the mail back on the coffee table, Sasha stood and walked out of the room to pack.

"You're unusually quiet."

"Just a little worn out."

"All that shopping and nightlife, huh?" Trey pulled away from the airport and headed toward the interstate. His fingers loosened on the steering wheel and even the stop-and-go traffic didn't dampen his mood. Just the scent of Sasha's perfume, the wide smile she'd aimed his way while walking out of the airport doors and the lingering heat of their kiss was enough to make his day.

"I wish you could have come. Lena would love you and her fiancé could have used the backup."

He placed his hand on her thigh and gave a little squeeze. "Want me to take you home?"

She shook her head and turned those baby brown eyes on him. It was all Trey could do to maintain his focus on driving. All he wanted to do was look at her.

"We could go to your place, light a few candles and curl up in the middle of that king-size bed of yours and I could use your body as my pillow," she said.

"Oh, yeah! Now that's what I'm talking about," Trey said with a grin. He hit the gas, his mind planning ahead. Twenty minutes to the building, three minutes from the garage to loft, two minutes to the bedroom, including stripping off her clothes.

"But I can't."

"What?" He swung his head to look at her face. "You're joking."

"Afraid not. I had a dozen messages from Jackson, the attorney, the foundation publicist and the zookeeper. I'm almost happy that the cell phone battery died so I don't feel compelled to call them back," she said and sighed.

"You can use my phone," Trey said.

"Trey," she said, her voice dropping. Whenever Sasha used that tone of voice, he felt like a teenage boy caught with a girlie magazine. "I need to see Darwin and Zaza."

For the first time since he'd met Sasha, Trey felt he was about to snap. Intense annoyance built in his gut and threatened to spill out his throat. He'd put in a ton of hours at the clinic, spent time at the gym and hung out with the fellas, but he'd still ended up taking cold showers almost every night.

He'd got out of the bed that morning with the thought of what he wanted to do with her when he got Sasha back to his place. Before heading to the office, he'd put together a nice little musical playlist with all of their favorite songs and he'd earmarked a nice bottle of red wine. In between seeing patients and going over paperwork, he'd arranged to have flowers delivered and a gourmet meal ready in the refrigerator. "I was just hoping that we could spend a little QT time together."

"QT time?"

He gave her a long intense look before answering, "Quality time."

Sasha's chin rose and herlips curled upward. "Ahh. I like the sound of that. And what would we do during this quality time?"

"Well, I can't explain it. I'd have to demonstrate."

Her hand moved to his jean-clad thigh. "Can quality time be shared at my place or is it location specific?"

Trey switched lanes and sped up as traffic started to flow. The warmth of her hand and the massaging sensation of her fingertips blew away all of his previous feelings of annoyance. At that moment with the fire in his belly heating up, he didn't care where they spent time together.

"All I need is for us to be alone," he replied.

In response to Sasha's throaty laughter and lingering kiss on his neck, Trey's foot inched down on the accelerator.

It was close to eleven o'clock when Sasha and Trey entered her bedroom. Jackson had fixed a homecoming dinner for her. For Sasha the meal, complete with three courses, desert and coffee had felt like it would never end. Each time Jackson went to the kitchen Trey had leaned over and whispered in her ear. During the first course, his hand had inched up her thigh; the second course had brought the cool sensation of his fingertips lightly moving over the small of her back.

After dinner, she took Darwin for a walk and Jackson retired to his apartment in the back. Finally, they were alone.

When she walked into her bedroom, Sasha gasped as she looked around. Scented candles lit the room and the sultry smell of jasmine and sandalwood perfumed the air. The soft sounds of a guitar played from the recessed ceiling speakers. "How… When did you manage to do this?"

"You were gone longer than you thought."

Sasha pulled off her tennis shoes and stepped into Trey's embrace. Laying her head against his chest, she inhaled and a feeling of rightness washed over her body. Everything seemed serene and peaceful. That was until his hands crept under her sweater and rubbed against her back. She looked up at Trey and stared deeply into his brown eyes and her breath caught in her chest. She loved the way he looked at her.

She reached up, entwined her arms around his neck, and gently stroked his nape. "The second I stepped in line at the airport to leave last week, I missed being in your arms. Every morning I opened my eyes, I imagined that you were by my side. And now that I'm home and in your arms with the music and candlelight, I almost feel like this is a dream."

Trey removed his hands from her back and cradled her face. He leaned down and slowly, thoroughly took possession of her mouth, nipping the sweet bow of her lips. When he pulled back, she gazed up at him from heavy-lidded eyes.

"Baby, it's not a dream. You feel way too good for this not to be real."

Sasha's mouth went dry as Trey took a step back and removed his shirt. His naturally smooth chest and tight stomach made everything in her body tense. She reached up with the intention of running her fingers over his chest, but he reached out and caught her hand and placed her fingers over his lips. His tongue darted out and licked the sensitive nubs. Sasha sucked in a breath.

"Like that?" His voice had dropped an octave, but there was a warmth behind it that made him seem even more sexy, even more intense.

"Oh, yes," she managed to respond.

He raised her arms over her head and then removed her blouse. Even with the cooler air washing over her skin, Sasha felt beads of sweat on her brow. He placed his hands behind her back and made short work of her bra. Then he trailed his fingertips down her back and cupped her bottom, bringing her full contact with his aroused body.

"See what you do to me?"

Sasha swallowed and nodded. "Take me to bed, Trey," she whispered. Instead, his mouth clamped down on hers in a kiss that blew away anything she'd ever experienced. Pure need seemed to spill from his lips and rain over her tongue. And before she knew it, they'd managed to rid one another of the rest of their clothing. With a flick of the wrist, he pulled back the comforter and eased her down onto the bed.

Sasha almost cried out with joy when he slid into bed

beside her. Nothing between them but skin, and he pulled her to him and kissed her forehead and while his hand stoked her breaths. His lips trailed kisses down her cheek, brushing across her lips. He lavished slow, hot, lingering kisses over her neck and then settled on her breasts.

His hands explored every inch of her body, inflaming her skin into goose bumps, and making her moan with need and excitement. And his mouth… Never in a million years would Sasha be able to look at Trey's lips without recalling each erotic kiss he placed on her skin. Her eyes fluttered closed and she moaned.

"Open your eyes for me, sweetheart." His voice was deep and rough.

As she struggled to breathe through the waves of pleasure rolling over her body, the fierce look of passion on Trey's face threatened to send her over the edge. Acting on an instinct older than time, she wrapped her herself around him, moved into him and gave herself over to the wonder of love.

Ten minutes, twenty or a half hour later, Trey opened his eyes and looked over at Sasha. Something that she'd said during their dinner still stuck in his mind. They'd begun speaking candidly about failed relationships, but at some mysterious point the course of the conversation had veered from shallow to deep waters. "It was him, wasn't it?" he asked.

"What?" Sasha mumbled. She'd just found that

perfect combination of not too hard, not too soft, not too cold and not too hot in the bed. With Trey's arm nestled around her stomach and post-climax relaxation riding up and down her spine, she felt wonderful. No, better than wonderful. Love filled her soul and threatened to seep out her pores.

"Kenneth is the one who broke your heart."

"Trey," she sighed as the afterglow of their lovemaking began to dim. "Do we have to talk about this, now?"

"Yes."

Sasha opened her eyes and realized that instead of peacefully falling asleep in Trey's embrace she would have to talk about past business. Staring up at the ceiling, she watched the candlelight patterns ripple across the spackle. "Fine. You're wrong. It wasn't Kenneth. We got close but his parents got closer. He couldn't deal with his father and I didn't fit into his family."

"Then who was it?"

"Why do you want to know?"

"Because I don't want to make the same mistakes, Sasha. Somebody, somewhere hurt you so badly that you've been hiding out in the wilderness ever since."

"That's not true," she said slowly

"Are you sure about that?"

Several heartbeats passed before she responded. "Maybe at one point and time I wanted to get away from a broken heart. But, Trey, I love my career and if I spend weeks outside of civilization to get the material

I need, then so be it. This has nothing to do with my love life."

She turned over on her side and carefully tucked the sheet under her arms. "Where is this coming from, Trey?"

Trey rubbed the back of his neck, trying to ease the tension as he recalled his meeting with Kenneth that morning. "He talked about you today. He said letting you go was one of the biggest regrets in his life."

Her eyes opened and Sasha turned to face Trey. "Kenneth said that?"

"Yes."

"And that's reason for the music and candles? Not that you missed me but that you're jealous?"

"Hell, yes. I mean no. I missed you like crazy, but I'm not about to lose my woman to somebody trying to resurrect the past."

"You can't lose something that doesn't belong to you, Trey."

"A few minutes ago you were moaning the opposite," he said.

Sasha levered herself up on her elbow and glared down at his handsome face. "I'm going to pretend that I didn't hear that."

"You can pretend anything you want, but don't for a second think that it's alright for you to spend time with him.

"Your body can't pretend that we didn't almost set

fire to these sheets." He softened his statement by reaching down and fingering her.

Still tender and sensitive, Sasha couldn't push back a moan. "Not fair," she protested.

"What's that old phrase? Nothing's fair in love and war."

Her expression grew serious. "Which is this, Trey? Love or war?"

Now it was his turn to fall silent. Trey stared at her for a moment, then reached out and gently brushed her cheek with his finger. "It's not war."

Trying to hide her disappointment, Sasha broke eye contact. "Then does that mean it's love?"

"You asked first. Only fair that you answer…unless you're afraid."

For Sasha, it was like standing next to the scorpion's cage all over again. Poised to face heartbreak for a second time. It would be so easy not to answer, so easy to deny the root of her feelings. But she repeated her choice and thus consciously decided to risk the pain. "First, I'm not afraid," she said softly. "Second, I know that I'm in love with you."

She sucked in a breath and faced him again. The look of pure surprise on his face almost made her burst into laughter.

"Cat got your tongue?" Sasha inquired.

"Did you just say what I think you said?"

"I said that I love you, Trey Blackfox. Correction, I've fallen in love with you. I'm not telling you this because I expect you to feel the same. I just want you to know."

"I…"

Quelling the sick feeling in her stomach, Sasha mustered a smile and placed her fingertips over his lips. "Just be with me tonight, Trey. I've dreamed of you in my bed for weeks and now I want to enjoy this moment."

She turned over to her back, wrapped his arm around her stomach and closed her eyes. Willing the tears not to come, she waited, listening to the sound of Trey's breathing. When sleep called her home, she wondered if she'd made a mistake.

Chapter 18

Saturday afternoon found Trey walking into the living room of Jared's four-bedroom town house.

"The last time you invited me over for a game, I ended up helping you build a dog house," Trey commented as he sat on Jared's suede sofa with a bowl of nachos in one hand and a beer in the other,

"It was good exercise, right? You know that siding was an excellent addition."

"Jared, who puts together a custom-built dog-house? You could have picked one up at a pet store for half the price."

"Man, you are tight with your money. If I didn't know that you could give a top NBA draft pick a run for his money with the portfolio comparison, I'd think you were a step away from middle class."

"J, you built a dog house with glass windows, a door, a kitchen and bedroom."

"Look, Big Boy's special."

"Yeah, the dog is special all right, as in *special needs*. He's twenty pounds overweight. Are you feeding him the stuff I prescribed?"

"I put it in his bowl. Did I tell you that he didn't eat for two days? Dog was on some kind of hunger strike. He's been on the new food for about two weeks. I took him to the pet store last week and got him on the scale. You'll never believe that he's already dropped three pounds."

Trey turned his head to look over the sofa in the direction of Bog Boy's dog bed. Sure enough, the Labrador retriever was stretched out on his side with his tongue hanging out.

Jared took a swig of his beer. "Come spring, all the females will be flocking to meet and greet."

"We got him fixed after he started spraying in the house, remember?"

Jared reached forward and picked up the remote control from the coffee table. He switched on the big screen television and flipped through channels until he came to a comedy station. "Yeah, saddest day of my life. I'll never forget the look of betrayal. Sometimes I catch him staring at me with this queer look on his face. Like he's remembering. Anyway, he may not be packing but Big Boy can still pull in the honeys. Just like his dad."

"So what's up?" Trey asked.

"Can't I have my best friend over for a beer without having an ulterior motive?"

"No, you can't, so if you don't want to quit the innocent act, I'm making an early departure from this party."

"Okay, okay. I've got something that I need your help with."

"Call the clinic's hotline. I'm officially off today," he responded automatically.

Most Saturdays would find Trey in the office hard at work, but since he'd met Sasha, spending Saturdays working up diagnoses didn't seem as appealing.

He'd spent the past week trying to find a way to define his feelings toward her. Not one to talk to other people, he'd caught himself asking advice from some of his animal patients. He'd tried to go on as though things hadn't changed since Sasha's return from New York, but he couldn't deny that without her with him at night, he couldn't sleep. That since knowing her, he felt incomplete.

"Look, every man who's got a house and a dog needs a pickup truck," Jared said.

"What?" Trey pulled his attention back to the present. "So you invited me over here to help you pick out a truck? All you have to do is drive up to Cartersville. My uncle Will could pull a nice one off the car lot for you," he said.

"Nah, you're not hearing what I'm trying to say. Getting a truck is only half of the equation—getting a wife is the other half."

Trey choked on his beer. "How the hell did you get from buying a car to getting hitched?"

"I'm not getting any younger and my house isn't feeling like a home. I'm going to ask my sister to help me go ring shopping next weekend. And I wanted to ask you in person if you'd be my best man."

Something punched Trey in the gut and did a vicious twist. He put down his beer and sat back on the sofa. While his eyes focused on the television screen, his mind was miles away. Seventeen to be exact. Everything and everyone was changing. The fact that Jared was about to propose just underscored that point. There would be no more random weekends just watching games, playing video games or hitting the basketball court. No more impromptu trips to Miami to attend sporting events or to babe watch. Then again, he didn't really want to see any other woman other than Sasha. And that sore spot felt like he'd just rubbed salt in the wound. Men would kill to have his seats, commit suicide to have his life and he was pining for a woman.

Jared snapped his fingers in front of Trey's eyes. "You all right, man? You kind of zoned out for a minute."

"You know how to catch a man off guard."

"Well, don't feel like the Lone Ranger. I wasn't expecting to have this conversation until I was at least forty. You know I wanted to be the last man standing and here I am the first one to go. But I don't mind. I can't think of living my life without her."

"She makes you that happy?"

"Yep."

Trey picked up his beer and inclined it in Jared's direction. "Well, partner, it looks like you've got a best man."

The incessant sound of the doorbell ringing roused Sasha from a light doze. Beams of sunlight formed random designs on the walls and floor. The house was very quiet. Sasha glanced at the clock and then rolled out of bed at the sound of knocking. Running a hand through her hair, she went downstairs to the front door unlocked and opened it not bothering to first take a look through the peek hole.

"About time you opened the door! I was about to call the police."

Her eyes widened and her mouth dropped open. "Mom...Dad. What are you doing here?"

"I don't know why your father's here," Mom answered, walking through the doorway. "But after listening to dozens of messages from friends, former colleagues and fellow researchers letting me know that my girl's been in every newspaper from here to China, I'm here to straighten this mess out."

An hour later, after installing her parents in one of the guest rooms, putting on clothes and making tea,

Sasha took a deep breath and sat down in a living room chair. Of all the reactions she'd expected from her parents, this hadn't been the one she'd anticipated. Then again, she hadn't expected her parents when she'd opened the door fresh from an erotic flashback of love-making with Trey and a morning of Belgian waffles and whipped cream. Sasha squashed the urge to blush at the thought of what she and Trey had done with the full can of whipped cream. The shower to rinse the stickiness from all of their unmentionable places had been just as wicked.

"I'm happy to see you."

"Well, I'm happy to see my daughter, but I'm not happy to see your picture in the newspaper under the caption 'Atlanta's Bachelorette.' I'm not happy that you didn't see fit to tell us that Camden named you as the sole heir to his estate and I'm not happy that you've given up your life's work to live in this life of moral depravity and capitalist selfishness," her father said.

"Arthur," her mother interjected.

"Daddy! I am not giving up my work. I just have to remain here to get some things sorted out. I'm pretty close to hiring a staff to oversee the foundation that's been set up in Uncle Camden's name and I need to find a home for the kittens. After that I should be able to resume my work in some capacity."

"Really?"

"Yes."

"Then you have no ties with Atlanta and those two men they talked about in the article aren't trying to put a ring on your finger?"

"I can assure you that Trey hasn't gone down on bended knee and Kenneth hasn't been to pick out a ring," she told her parents.

"Baby girl, it really doesn't matter to us about the who, what, when or where. We are just concerned about you. This is a lot on your shoulders and I wish you'd come to us sooner."

"How could I? I didn't want to put a strain on your relationship. I remember what happened the last time," Sasha said.

"What do you mean you remember what happened the last time?"

"I heard you fighting, Dad."

"I thought—" her mother began.

"You thought I was asleep. I wasn't and even if I'd slept through the whole thing, you could have taken a machete to the tension between the two of you for weeks after you found out that Uncle Camden had funded my scholarships."

"See. The man wasn't happy with messing with me the first time. Now he has to mess with me after he's gone. He's getting his revenge from the grave."

"Why would Uncle Camden want revenge?"

Her parents looked at one another and her father's lips pressed together in a thin line. Sasha repeated slowly, "Why would Uncle Camden want revenge?"

"Because he was always in love with your mother."

Sasha's stomach dropped to the floor. She sat back stunned. "Mom?"

"Oh, baby. It's true.

"It wasn't something that we ever spoke about. He never said anything and he always treated me with respect."

"I just thought…"

"That he was like a brother to your father. It has always been that way. He knew that I could never return his affection.

"Then how do you know this?"

Her father spoke up. "He told me one night. We were in a German pub knocking back way too many beers. I don't remember how we got there, don't remember how we got back to the hotel. But I'll never forget seeing him staring down at the half-filled glass, shoulders slumped, looking like a man with no home, no hope, no peace."

"And you didn't say anything?" Sasha asked.

"What could I do? What could I say to the man who was in love with my wife? He was like a brother to me. I did the only thing I could and ordered another round."

"I refuse to believe that Uncle Camden made me his heir out of revenge."

"I, as well," her mother responded.

"I knew you would take her side."

"There are no sides in this, Arthur. Even you can't

deny that Camden loved Sasha, loved her as the daughter he never had."

"You mean the daughter that he couldn't have because he was in love with you."

Her mother's face turned as if she'd been slapped. The air rushed of Sasha's lungs.

"I'm sorry. I didn't mean it."

Her mother stood and then held up a single finger. "Don't talk to me, Arthur."

Sasha sat rooted to her seat as her mother turned and looked at her. "Butterfly, I need to get out of here before I say something to your father that I'll regret."

"Where are you going to go? You can't drive."

The air left Sasha's lungs in a whoosh at her father's snide remark. Yes, she'd overheard her parents arguing before, but she'd never seen her father behave in such a hateful manner.

"I can walk and I can still dial a phone."

Sasha leaped from her seat and grabbed her mom's arm. "Mom, why don't I take you upstairs so you can rest? You always said traveling wears you out."

"That's too close. I need to be miles, not yards from your father."

"Leave your mother alone. I'll drive you where you want to go."

"No, thank you," her mother practically spat.

Sasha let out a sigh of resignation. "Just let me get the keys, Mom. I'll meet you in your room in ten minutes."

It took her two minutes to locate the phone and twenty seconds to dial Trey's number. Her evening plans had gone down in a ball of flames the moment the doorbell had rung that afternoon.

Trey was just stepping out of the shower when the phone rang.

"Trey."

"Hello, beautiful, how did you know that I was hoping to hear your sweet sexy voice?"

"Great minds think alike."

"I really wanted to wake you up just to see you smile."

"I think it was for the best, Trey. I'm sorry but I can't see you for a few days."

He finished drying off and headed into the closet. "Oh, well, we're still on for my grandfather's birthday party, right? My mother won't let me come home unless I've got you on my arm."

"I won't be able to make that, either."

Trey was so startled he let go of his towel. "What's happened?" he demanded after reaching over and grabbing a pair of black slacks.

"My parent showed up on my doorstep."

"I thought you said your parents live in Cuba."

"They do. Someone showed them a picture of us at the zoo exhibit party."

"And... There's a perfectly respectable picture of us in the newspaper. I'm not seeing the problem."

"I didn't tell them about you. And if you read the article you'll see that the reporter called me 'Atlanta's Millionaire Bachelorette.' I hadn't told them about the inheritance yet, either."

Things clicked into place as Trey recalled some of the snippets of conversations when Sasha had described her parents. From what he'd gleaned, Dr. Arthur Clayton wouldn't react well to finding out his daughter was keeping secrets. "Damn. I'll be right over."

"No, you won't. I got myself into this situation— I'll resolve it. I should have told them about all of this a long time ago."

"You shouldn't go through this alone."

"I'll be fine. It's just my parents."

"You sure?" he asked. The sense of fragility and sadness in her voice pulled at his gut. He wanted to throw on his clothes and race over there and do whatever it took to make her smile.

"Positive."

"I'll check on you later," Trey stated. "If you need me call my cell phone and if I don't pick up call the office."

"I'll be okay."

"Promise to call me," he repeated. "If you don't I'm going to be on my way over before you can hang up the phone."

"I promise," she replied and he caught a hint of a smile in her voice. "I've got to go."

The line went dead. Trey clicked the off button on

the phone and stared at it for a moment. Sasha was in trouble, but she didn't want his help. He thought about the situation for a moment and uncertainty twisted in his stomach. What kind of man was he that his woman couldn't depend on him? More importantly, how would he be able to keep the love of his life if her esteemed father hated his guts?

After a hard day of not only seeing his appointments, but working the emergency in-take, as well, Trey was ready for some downtime. But once behind the wheel of his SUV, he'd started having flashbacks of Sasha's scent, her little moans and whimpers, the way she'd done a little shimmy shake leading up to her climax. Instead of going home, he'd driven to her place. Now he slowly pulled into the mansion's circular driveway and parked in front of the entranceway.

He removed his seat belt, put his keys in his jacket pocket and he looked over at the shoebox sitting in the leather passenger seat. Sure enough, a little black and white head rose over the top to stare at him. He'd been a practicing vet for over five years and could boast that he'd never taken his work home.

Until now.

His last patient of the day lay curled up in the temperature-controlled confines of his vehicle. Named Ralph by one of the assistants, the little miniature boxer and three of his siblings had been abandoned in the clinic parking lot. The puppy inched forward and Trey was compelled to reach over and stroke him on the head. "I only need to run in for a minute. A half hour at the most."

Black protruding eyes just continued to stare at him. Trey pulled back and turned and pulled on the door handle only to freeze as the puppy let out a small whimper.

Trey shut the door, sat back and returned his attention to Ralph. "Look, you don't want to go in there with me. There's my girlfriend, her parents, a Jack Russell terrier, a Persian cat about five times your size, not to mention a British butler, in there."

Uncaring, Ralph whined again. "You just went to the bathroom before we left."

The puppy stood on his wobbly legs and whimpered again, this time a little louder. "For being the runt of the litter you sure do have strong vocal cords. You're supposed to be conserving your energy."

Trey scooped Ralph up with one hand and placed him against his sweater, then zipped up his leather jacket. The dog's little legs wiggled a bit, then he settled down and rested his face against Trey's chest. Unconsciously a grin sprang up on Trey's face. As he cupped his hands under Ralph's rear end, he caught the slight sound of a tiny snore. He looked down to see the puppy's closed eyes and open mouth. "You picked a great time to go to sleep. I might need your help in there, so don't get too comfortable."

He jumped out of the car and rang the doorbell, hoping that Sasha would be the one greeting him at the door. Instead the door swung back to reveal a T-shirt-and-shorts wearing Jackson. Trey fought the urge to shiver. Just looking at the other man's pale legs made him clutch the puppy tighter.

Jackson caught his movement and narrowed his eyes. "I'm leaving for the airport within the hour."

"Where are you headed?"

"Jamaica."

"When will you be back?"

"The day after Arthur Clayton departs to his beloved Cuba."

Trey scanned the area before responding, "Sasha's father is that bad?"

"I shall tell you that Sasha's mother is the essence of a lady—good humor, well mannered, intelligent and likable. Her husband, on the other hand, is a narrow-minded bigot with a distain for those who live above poverty level."

"So are her parents around?"

"They're settled in the back guest room arguing. If you'd like to speak to Sasha, I suggest you hurry upstairs."

"Thanks."

"She has Darwin and Zaza with her so you might not want to let the puppy run loose."

Trey nodded and headed for the stairs. He stopped and turned on the third step. "Hey, Jackson."

"Yes."

"Have a good trip."

Trey took the stairs two at a time until he reached the landing. Then walking as softly as he could, he located Sasha's bedroom door and tapped. The door swung open and Sasha peeked out. Her eyes widened. "Trey, what are you doing here?"

"Checking up on you."

Between one blink and the next, she grabbed his arm and pulled him inside. "Easy, sweetheart."

She closed the door and leaned against it. "I don't want my parents to see you."

He looked her over from head to toe and even covered in flannel, she was beautiful. "They can't be that bad."

"Dad thinks you're an eccentric playboy who's going to break my heart after leading me down the path to capitalist purgatory."

"He got all that from a picture?"

"And some digging around on the Internet. He had a blast reciting all the names of your numerous ex-flames."

Trey winced. "I think you're right about that not meeting the parents."

He watched as her gaze left his. "Trey, why is your chest moving?" Sasha asked.

Startled. He quickly lowered the zipper on his jacket to show Ralph's little head.

Sasha took two steps forward and cooed. "Oh, he's adorable."

"Ralph's the runt of the litter that someone dropped

at the clinic's front door last night. Most of the puppies are in good health and we're pretty confident that once they're weaned, we'll be able to get them into good homes."

"You're going to keep him?"

"No…no. I'm just making sure that there aren't any complications from the medication."

"Really?" She smiled as though she were humoring him.

"Jo had a family emergency and couldn't make the night rounds."

"If you say so," Sasha said, and then took another step closer to Trey. He inhaled the scent of her perfume and his body temperature shot up at least five degrees.

"He's so cute and he doesn't seem like he'd be any trouble. I'd take him if Darwin wasn't such a handful."

Trey looked down at the sleeping puppy and his gut lurched, but he fought it. "Don't let the innocent look fool you. He sucks down milk like a baby walrus and he makes some nasty poop."

Sasha laughed and reached out to run a finger over Ralph's tiny head. Unbidden, his heart melted at the gentle loving expression on her face. He wished she would look at him like that instead of the canine asleep on his chest.

"I'm sure he'll grow up to be a charmer like his vet."

Forgetting that her parents were less than a hundred

feet away, Trey leaned forward and gave in to the urge to kiss her lips. "So you think I'm charming, huh?"

"You have your moments."

"How about now."

"With the puppy, you are one-hundred-percent pure sexy."

"For real."

"Uh-huh."

"Well, can I trade some of my sexiness for another kiss?" he asked.

Too busy listening to his heartbeat and tasting the sweetness of her kiss, that sound of the tapping against the door went in one ear and out the other, skipping the cognizant portion of his brain.

"I knocked, butterfly, but you didn't answer. Your father and I talked."

"What the—" The sound of an outraged voice pulled him from the fog of desire.

Sasha turned around and stood in front of Trey. "Mom, Dad, this isn't what you think."

"You're right about that." Her father stormed forward, glaring at Trey. "I don't think there's a man in your bedroom—I know he's here."

Her mother moved forward and placed a restraining hand on her father's shoulder. "Arthur, calm down. Sasha is a grown woman and this is her house. She's entitled to have company."

Sasha never took her eyes off her father. Trey

examined the man. Standing at a good five feet eleven inches, Arthur Clayton commanded respect.

"Thank you, Mother. Now that you've embarrassed us all. I'll skip ahead to the introductions."

"I know who you are. What I want to know is what you're doing in my baby girl's bedroom knowing that her parents are down the hall? Didn't your parents teach you any manners or did your nanny miss that chapter in the 'How to raise rich kids' manual?"

"Daddy, be nice."

Determined not to rise to the bait, Trey held out his right hand while cradling Ralph with his left. "I'm here because I care about your daughter and wanted to check on her and I'm holding out my hand to you in friendship because I was raised to respect my elders regardless of the situation."

For a second, Trey thought Mr. Clayton would leave him hanging, but after a minute, he shook his hand.

He turned to Mrs. Clayton and put on his best smile. "It's a pleasure to finally meet Sasha's mother. She's spoken about you often and I can finally see where she gets her beauty from."

Mrs. Clayton's brow rose but her lips inched upward in a smile. Instead of taking his hand she moved forward and enfolded him in a light hug, then moved back to examine Ralph. "I don't know which is more adorable, you or the puppy."

"I agree, Mom. They're more like double trouble." Sasha chuckled. "How about we go down to the kitchen and I can see if I can figure out how to use the coffee machine and fix us all a cup."

"I'm sorry but I can't stay."

"Is that right."

"But there's something else I need to do before I go. I wanted to extend an invitation to your parents. Mr. and Mrs. Clayton, I can understand that you're anxious about me and your daughter's new situation. I'd like to invite you to my grandfather's birthday celebration this weekend. It would be the perfect opportunity for us to get to know one another better and you can meet my family."

"We'd—" Mr. Clayton began.

Mrs. Clayton jabbed an elbow in her husband's stomach. "We'd love to."

"Great. I'll come by on Saturday morning. We've got lots of room at the house and Mom loves to have guests."

He started inching toward the door and made an excuse. "I need to get home before Ralph's next feeding. Sasha, will you walk me out?"

"Of course."

They didn't say a word until reaching the bottom stair. "That didn't go well."

"Are you kidding? My parents just weren't speaking to each other before you arrived. I just found out that Uncle Camden was in love with my mother. At least now they'll have something else to argue about."

"So you're not angry?""

"About?"

"The party. I was going to ask you last night but I was distracted."

"By our chess match?"

He smiled. "You've got a pair of pieces that kept me from thinking straight."

"No, I don't mind. It'll be great to see your mother again and hopefully it will help my father dig himself out of the prejudiced hole he's dug himself into."

Chapter 19

Two days later when Sasha opened the bedroom door at his parents' house, Trey had to take a step back. God, she was beautiful with her black hair down and her large brown eyes shining. After the previous weekend of lovemaking, he should have been be sated or at least in more control of his libido.

He wasn't. If they didn't have his grandfather's celebration to attend, and if her parents hadn't shown up at Sasha's doorstep, he'd ask her to shimmy out of the burgundy dress and play doctor.

He reached out, took her hand, and softly kissed the back. "You look like heaven."

"I look like a TV show makeover project," she responded. "I'm not sure I'm going to be able to get through the night without breaking my neck on these heels or passing out with embarrassment when my father goes into one of his anticapitalism tirades."

Trey laughed at the thought of that. He gently coaxed her farther into the hallway and shut the door, just so that he wouldn't have to look at the temptation of the nicely made up bed.

"Do you like the bedroom?"

"It's lovely."

"It was mine."

Her eyes widened with disbelief. "I can't say that the design is your style."

"It isn't. Once we all were kicked out of house, my mother donated all the furniture and put everything else away in the storage room off the basement. I'm sure she's going to make a special trip down there to dig out baby pictures to humiliate me."

"Good," she said in an extremely cheerful tone. "I can't wait to see them. You might have been a spoiled rotten brat as a child, but I'm sure you were just as handsome."

Trey couldn't resist leaning down and kissing her. Not a peck on the cheek. He kissed her softly and gently, tracing his tongue over the outside of her lips before drawing back and leaving both of them breathless.

A confident grin took over his face at the sight of Sasha's dilated eyes. He felt like the king of the world just because he was the only one who could have that effect on her. "I might have to talk to your mother about getting some pictures of you, as well." He chuckled.

Sasha scowled. "Over my dead body. I wasn't a photogenic kid."

"I'd like to be the judge of that."

"I'm sure you would. But before you try to con my mother out of the pictures, we may want to stop by a bathroom."

"Why?"

She laughed softly. "Because copper brown just isn't your color and I probably look like I put my lipstick on in the dark."

Any member of the Blackfox family could have walked down the upstairs hallway. Still, he wanted to reach over and take her into his arms. To bury his face against the curve of her neck and inhale that sultry perfume of hers. There was something about her that attracted him. Made him ache and yet at the same time softened him.

Trey pulled a handkerchief from his pocket, and wiped his lips. "Speaking of bathrooms, I'll probably disappear in about an hour to check on Ralph."

"Are you sure you should leave the puppy in your sister's cottage by himself?"

"Last I checked he was all nice and curled up on one of my old sweatshirts in the bathroom. If he has an accident, I have a gallon of bleach on standby. But he's a good boy. He'll go on the puppy pads."

She smiled. "It almost sounds like you're fond of him."

"You can't help but to like the little guy. He's got spunk."

"So you're going to keep him?"

A negative response sprang to his lips but didn't come out of his mouth. The truth be told when it came to giving the canine to his future adopted parents, he knew that he'd be reluctant to let Ralph go. Since bringing him home from the clinic, the puppy had been a constant companion. He'd even managed to sneak into his coat pocket and tag along during patient appointments. He liked having the dog, but he had to put Ralph's needs before his own and with his schedule and living arrangements, it just wouldn't work. "I can't keep him."

"Why not?"

"I keep crazy hours between the clinic and the zoo. Ralph needs a stable environment with a family and kids."

"All that puppy needs is love and attention and who better than his own personal vet. I bet he's the healthiest runt you've ever seen."

Trey shrugged his shoulders. "I made sure that he gets his vitamins and an extra serving of formula. But that doesn't qualify me for pet ownership."

"You're going to fight this until the very end, aren't you?"

"Aren't you?" he parried back. He didn't believe that

for a moment she was completely settled into her new life in Atlanta. Her parents' arrival and the heated debate in the car on their drive up that morning had made it all the more evident that Sasha continued to have misgivings.

She shook her head. "Touché. I'm working on my issues, though."

"Well, I'm keeping mine for a while. So are you ready to get the party started?"

She pulled her hand from his and turned. "Let's go."

They reached the end of the hallway and as he moved to descend to the main floor, Sasha paused.

Sighing with irritation, Trey backed up a step. "What's wrong?" he asked.

"I'm nervous." She looked out over the mass of guests.

"About meeting the rest of my family?"

"No, I don't deal well in social situations and this place easily has over fifty people and I don't do so well with people."

"Stay close to me and it'll be okay."

"Trey, what fool went off and let this beautiful lamb in your paws?"

Sasha glanced over to see a handsome man walking in their direction. After meeting Trey's grandfather, she easily recognized the high cheekbones, light eyes and curly black hair so much like the family patriarch.

"Marius," Trey growled. "Not tonight."

He placed an empty glass on a passing waiter's tray. "What? Tonight's for family. Now don't be rude. Introduce me to the lady you must have paid half your trust fund to be your date."

"Sasha Clayton. This is my brother, Marius."

"Charmed," Marius said and took her hand within both of his own.

"Great. Now don't you have to go and play big shot or something?" Trey asked.

"Nope. Dad's got everything covered."

"Didn't your cell phone just ring? It could be an emergency at the plant."

Marius deliberately widened his eyes. Sasha covered her mouth to hide a laugh.

"Left my cell phone in the truck, bro. It's looking like you're trying to get rid of me," Marius said.

"I am," Trey responded pointedly.

"He's afraid you'll spill all of his secrets." Sasha laughed.

Marius crooked his arm. "Let me order you a drink and I'll tell you everything you want to know."

Before Trey could open his mouth to protest, Sasha placed her arm on Marius's biceps and slipped from his side.

"Close your mouth, son. People might think you've lost your mind."

"Dad, did you see that?" His head swung around like the possessed girl in an old exorcist movie.

"Yep. That oldest of mine is smooth. Must have been

paying attention when I told all of you how to treat a lady."

Trey rubbed his brow and concentrated on not staring in the direction Sasha had gone. "What do you think?

"About Sasha or her parents?"

"Both."

"She's one-of-a-kind, loyal, classic kind of lady that I hope you don't mess around and lose. Her parents are good people. Different, but the kind that would fit into our clan. You mother and I could tell that they don't care for money, and her father and I don't see eye to eye on politics, but he loves his family so he's all right by me."

The knot of tension he hadn't known he'd possessed unfurled at this father's implicit blessing. The thing was that he agreed with his father's assessment of Sasha. She was a special woman. The question was if she was that one women for him. Was she the woman that meant it was time to toss out his black book? He looked down at his fingers and began to count off. The sex was phenomenal, she wasn't after his money, he enjoyed the hell out of spending time with her, they shared the same interests, his mother loved her, and if that didn't beat all, she'd never bore him and she could play a mean game of chess.

His brother came along side and leaned up against the wall with a drink in this hand.

"Come on, Trey. She's sexy as hell, has a thing for

animals and isn't after your wallet. What else do you need?" Caleb paused, then looked over where half of the Blackfox women were standing. "Seriously, little brother. If Sasha isn't the one for you, then can you step aside and let another brother try to get happily-ever-after?"

"Touch her, Caleb, and you might wake up with a baby python on your pillow." His brother went pale at the mere mention of a snake. During one of their yearly sojourns to summer camp in Macon, someone forgot to close the cabin door. After coming back from a late night bathroom run, Caleb had sat down on his bunk bed and pulled back his blanket to discover that he had company. A nice-size copperhead snake had taken up residence in his absence. Trey would never forget the shout of terror that had woken him in the middle of the night. He burst out laughing at the image of Caleb running from the room in his Superman undershorts.

Caleb's nose twitched to the side. "That's not funny."

"Oh, yet it is. I've seen a lot of things but that's the only time that I've seen a black man turn white. You were practically albino."

"If you don't want to talk about your woman, than all you had to say was back off."

Trey finished off a vodka tonic. "Back off."

"All right."

Marius stepped forward and put a hand on Trey's shoulder. Trey eyed his eldest brother suspiciously. "So who gets to be the best man?"

Trey crossed his eyes and refused to give into the urge to go back to his room and hit the bed. Instead, he singled to the bartender for another glass. When it came he took a deep drink, and the warm liquid gave him a welcome artificial calm. "There isn't going to be a wedding. And even it I was thinking about getting hitched, you two would be the last people in the world I'd choose."

"That hurt." Caleb grabbed his chest and pretended to be wounded. "But it's okay. You're my brother so I'll forgive you."

Trey inclined his head over to the far right where a statuesque woman appeared to be in deep conversation with his grandparents. "Tell it to Amber because she's free of husband number one and I heard she's plans in the works for number two."

Marius caught Trey's sly wink and ran with the joke. "Yeah, I heard that she's looking for an emergency room doctor with unlimited access to Viagra and a black American Express card."

"Oh, ya'll want to talk about hearing things, huh? What about our little jailbird here?" Caleb pointed at Trey.

Grinding his teeth at the memory of that night, Trey stared helplessly at his older brother. A minute ago, a police officer would have sworn on a stack of bibles that Marius was legally intoxicated. But the way he drew himself up and narrowed his eyes erased that notion.

"What?" Marius barked.

Caleb looked back and forth between the two brothers and snickered. "Trey didn't tell you that he got arrested at a strip club?"

Marius's hand shot up and a small portion of his bourbon on the rocks hit the floor. "You got arrested at a strip club? Damn it, do you have any idea of what could have happened if the media had gotten a hold of that kind of information?"

Trey had barely opened his mouth before the unique scent of Sasha's perfume reached his nose.

"Strip club?"

The sound of Sasha's voice congealed the blood in his veins and stopped his heart with guilt. Apparently sometime during their conversation she'd come to stand by his side.

"Trey, you were arrested at a strip club?" Her voice wobbled with disbelief.

"No. Technically I was in the parking lot."

Trey wanted to shoot Caleb as he watched Sasha's lips purse and the muscles around her nose wrinkled with disapproval. "Was this before or after ogling naked women?"

"It was at a bachelor party. I couldn't say no to one of my friend's last nights of freedom, could I?"

The situation went form bad to worse as his mother joined the group. "Sasha, dear, why are you upset?"

Trey felt another moment of blind panic and instead of reacting by smooth talking his way out the situation, he hurriedly took another drink and prayed for divine intervention. When his mother aimed an expectant glance his way, he spoke up. "Nothing, Mom. Just having a friendly disagreement."

Her eyebrows shot up. Trey sent a pleading look toward Sasha.

"Is that true?" his mother asked, looking at Sasha for confirmation.

"Yes. Trey thinks that it's too feminine to join the women's walk for breast cancer."

"No... No... Not me. It was Caleb."

Caleb jumped to attention from his previous snickering. "Not me. Trey thought it was a waste of time."

Marius took advantage of his mother's attention being focused on Trey to sneak away from the group.

"No, what we meant was that we would walk and donate, sweetheart." Trey reached out, took her hand, and drew Sasha next to him. Her back was as unbending as an ironing board.

"That's my boys. Always willing to help." His mother smiled and Trey could breathe again. Something about being back in the house he grew up in made him feel like a kid instead of a grown man. On the other hand, maybe it was being in the presence of all his family members. In any case, the look of disappointment in Sasha's eyes made him feel like an ashamed five-year-old.

His mother patted Trey on the arm. "Sign both your grandmother and I up. Better yet, tell Marius to have the company do a sponsorship."

She turned toward Caleb. "Go find your aunt Mary. She's been having problems with her stomach."

Her attention then moved back to Trey. "You need to see Wilbur before you leave tomorrow. That old German shepard of your uncle's got bit by something this morning and your uncle refuses to take the dog to the vet."

"You, young lady, come with me. There are a lot of people I want you to meet."

"Breast walk for cancer," Caleb practically spat. "You might as well kiss my reputation bye-bye."

Trey put his hand on Caleb's slumped shoulders. "Look on the bright side. At least this will get Amber off your back."

Damn, he was a first-rate idiot. It was after three o'clock in the morning, but Trey was still awake mulling over the night's events. He should have grabbed Sasha and taken her to a quiet place and explained exactly what happened at the strip club and that he'd gotten the charges dismissed. But then she'd have been even more mad at him. Women could be so unpredictable. She already thought his morals were shaky because of his privileged childhood. The last thing he needed was to give her even more reasons to despise him.

Even as that thought finished, he thought of what Sasha would look like spitting mad. What she would look like with face flushed and tousled hair as he straddled her.

Growling, Trey pushed back the covers and almost tripped on his pants as he got out of bed. His balance unsteady by the countless glasses of whiskey he'd imbibed that night, he managed to pull on a pair of pants, a sweater, socks and shoes. Ten minutes later after making his way to the main house, Trey stood outside his little sister Regan's bedroom door and gently touched his head to the cool wood. It was humiliating to be sneaking around his parents' house. But he had little choice since his parents had put him in the guest cottage.

He tapped on the door with his finger twice. "Sasha, sweetheart, wake up."

Trey pressed his ear to the door and waited a moment for a response. He tapped again and whispered, "Baby, we need to talk. Just open the door."

He gently tried but found it locked. "It's not what it sounded like." His speech slurred slightly. "I went to the strip club for a friend's bachelor party. Why are you acting like I'm a pervert or something? Yes, I understand it's degrading for women. Trust me I didn't go there to degrade anybody. Just to celebrate a friend's last night of freedom and now I've got to pay a fine for brawling in public. So I've learned my lesson. What else can I say?"

The door opened and Trey's sight of the person coming out the room shocked him into instant sobriety. "Mrs. Clayton!"

"Keep your voice down." She pushed him farther

back into the hallway and closed the door. "You better be really happy my husband is a heavy sleeper."

"I apologize. I thought you were Sasha."

"Really," she said dryly. "She's down the hall. And now I know why my baby barely said a word tonight."

"It's just a misunderstanding."

"Trey, can I be honest with you?"

Standing in the hallway of his family home at four o'clock in the morning, straight busted. He needed some truth. "Please."

"You're going to have to make up your mind and you'll need to do it fast. I like you and I think that you and your family are wonderful for my daughter. My husband, on the other hand, doesn't feel the same way. Sasha loves her Daddy and will walk off the ends of the earth if that man asks. If you love her, and I do think that you do, get your act together, patch things up and show that stubborn man I married that he's wrong to think that you're Don Juan incarnate."

With that she patted him on the cheek and disappeared back into the bedroom.

For several moments, Trey just stood there looking at the door, then he started toward the first floor.

"If you love her…"

Mrs. Clayton's words echoed in his head. Did he love her? He looked at where he was and what he'd done and how he felt and there was no other answer than yes. What kind of man does this kind of stuff? Either a fool or a man in love.

Chapter 20

Sasha stepped out of the grocery store and into the parking lot. The temperature had to be in the forties but the cool air felt wonderful against her flushed cheeks. She hadn't slept well at all last night. Finding out that Trey had been arrested outside a strip club had only served to intensify her misgivings about the relationship. Everything her father had said about the behavior of rich people kept echoing in her mind. Trey's family seemed to act like normal people even if they did enjoy a grander lifestyle.

After stowing the bag of groceries in the back, Trey opened the passenger-side door. Ignoring the nicety, she climbed in and put on her seat belt.

Trey released a loud sigh. "Look, Sasha, if this relationship is going to have a future, you can't just leave and then subject me to the silent treatment whenever we get into a disagreement."

She really didn't want to have this conversation and she'd done her best to avoid speaking with Trey altogether after the birthday celebration. Yes, she was angry that he went to a strip club, but she was more upset about the larger implications of his actions. After the events of that weekend, she could no longer ignore the fact that although she had chosen Trey to be the one she wanted for a lifetime, he wasn't ready.

"I didn't storm out and we were not having a disagreement," she snapped once he'd gotten into the car. "We were in the middle of a party and I didn't want to embarrass either on of us by voicing what I thought about your getting arrested at a strip club."

"I was outside of the strip club trying to keep the peace."

"Apparently the police thought otherwise."

"That was until they heard the whole story. I wasn't even put into a holding pen. Caleb told me that they took me straight to the hospital for evaluation and that's where he picked me up. Once my attorney files the papers the charges will be dropped."

"Just like that?"

"Yes. I don't know why you're making such a big deal about it. I barely watched the show."

"Okay, Trey. Let's flip the situation. How would

you feel if I dressed up in sexy lingerie?" She leaned down, and then pretended to draw up a pair of imaginary stocking. "Put on my highest heels and let a group of half naked men dance for me."

His teeth clenched at the thought of Sasha seeing any man's body but his own. For one second he wanted to spit nails, but the triumphant look in her eyes stopped him. "You've proved your point," he growled.

"Good."

"So now what? Where do we go from here?"

"Home. I need you to take me home," she said slowly.

"And afterwards?"

"You go off to your little cave and think."

His brows wrinkled. "Think about what?"

"In all the time that we've been together, we've never spoken about the future. I've never asked you to make promises or commitments."

"That's true."

"Well, I can't do it anymore. Nature has a cycle. We humans have a cycle. We're born, we grow up, we fall in love, get married, have children and retire. I can't tell myself that just being with you is enough. It's a lie." Her voice trailed off and she stared out the window. "Uncle Camden loved my mother enough to let her go, but I'm not that strong."

"Look, sweetheart, I don't think I'm ready for marriage. I probably won't be there for ten years."

She'd told him she wanted to marry him, and he'd

said he didn't want to get married for another decade. She guessed that it was better than an outright rejection. "So you love me but not enough to make a commitment?"

"I have made a commitment to you, sweetheart. You've got my heart."

"For how long? What's going to happen next month when you go on a business trip? A year from now? What about five years from now? How long do I wait for you? How long do I close my eyes and blindly hope that one morning you'll wake up and realize that you can't live without me?"

"Why are you getting all worked up over nothing?" He stomped on the brakes and threw the car into Park. "Did my mother pressure you into this?"

"No. This is all me. I spent an hour talking with your grandmother. She's a wonderful woman who's been married to your grandfather for over fifty years."

"My grandmother put you up to this, didn't she?" he asked. "She's been dying for one of us to have a baby. "

Sasha reached for the door handle. "Unlock the door, Trey."

"Not until you tell me what I can do to fix this?"

"Show me that you don't just love me now when I'm in the prime of my life. Make me trust that you'll love me when I'm old, menopausal, heavyset and cranky. Make me believe that love can last a lifetime."

He shook his head and he pressed the button to unlock the doors. She yanked the door open and climbed out before the tears came rushing from her eyes. As Sasha walked, she scrambled to pull the keys from her purse, almost dropping them. She turned and glanced through the beveled glass and caught a glimpse of him pulling out of the driveway before her vision blurred and she reached up to wipe away the tears.

She'd come to Atlanta to carry out her uncle's last will and testament, not to fall in love with a man who wasn't ready to fully commit to loving her

"Baby, I can't take it anymore. I have to say something before we leave."

"What is it, Mom?"

"You're miserable."

She managed a half smile. "Of course I'm sad. You're leaving in the morning."

"Butterfly, this is the woman who's changed your diapers and did your hair for prom. I can tell when you're lying and I can tell when your heart is breaking."

"Breaking, broken." She shrugged and took a seat on the window seat. "What's the difference? I'll get over it."

Her mother paused while putting on a pair of silver earrings. "Will you?"

Sasha looked away from her mother and wouldn't let herself cry. It had been three days since Trey had driven right out of her life. She'd put on a brave face and told her parents their break up was for the best. But her insides still churned from the thought that she would spend the rest of her life missing him, loving him. Her parents' presence was the only thing that kept her from crawling into bed and hiding under the covers.

"No," she whispered softly as the image of her mother blurred from the tears in her eyes. "I'm not going to get over this for a long time."

Her mother turned, crossed the room and sat next to Sasha. "Butterfly, you don't have to do this. Go to Trey and talk this through."

"What's there to talk about? I can't make him fall in love with me."

"I agree. Even a fool can see that he's in love with you and your father may be many things but he's not a fool. He realizes that Trey loves you."

"Really?"

She nodded. "Yes. He might not like Trey's financial status, his political affiliations or his family's wealth, but he knows that the man would put your needs and welfare above his own. And in the end, that's all a father wants for his daughter."

"She's right, you know."

Sasha looked up to see her father standing in the doorway. "Daddy, how long have you been standing there?"

"Long enough to tell you that your mother missed a few things. I don't agree with Trey's taste in music, either, but the man has impeccable taste in coffee."

"I thought you'd given up caffeine."

"A sip now and then can't hurt."

Sasha stood up and gave her father a quick hug. "We

should be getting ready to go to the aquarium, not standing here talking about something that doesn't matter."

Arthur reached out and laid a hand on her arm. "No, it matters. I don't want you throwing away a chance at happiness because of my pigheadedness."

Sasha's brow furrowed. "Daddy?"

"I was wrong in my decision to cut Camden off from my life. I was wrong to let my pride get the better of me and I'm going to regret it until the day I die. But I don't want you to make my mistake. If you truly love the man and feel that you can start a life with him, you have my blessing."

Sasha hung her head and shut her eyes, but nothing could have stopped the tears from escaping her closed lids. She hiccupped, as the air seemed stuck in her chest. She collapsed into her father's arms and sobbed. What did it matter that she had her father's approval when the man she loved didn't love her back?

Chapter 21

Trey sat forward in his courtside seat and stared forward instead of watching the player run to the other end of the Phillips Arena basketball court. The roar of the crowd with the action hot and time ticking away couldn't pull him out of the funk he'd fallen in since he'd last seen Sasha. He'd sent her roses and chocolate only to get back an envelope with the platinum ankle bracelet he'd given her to celebrate their one month anniversary.

"All right, Trey. I've had enough."

He turned and looked at Jared. "Enough of what?"

"Look, just apologize, beg, lie, bribe. Hell, I'll even beg for you but you have got to get Sasha back because you're making me miserable," Jared said.

"Now wait a minute," Trey said heatedly, forgetting for a moment at he'd promised to enjoy himself. "I'm not miserable. My team is winning and I'm about to collect on our bet."

"Trey." The look Jared gave him only irritated him further.

"What?" he said tersely.

"Look at the scoreboard."

With a sinking feeling in his gut, he turned and looked. The Hawks were up against the Bulls by twenty points. He looked farther to the left and saw that it was the fourth quarter with five minutes left in the game. He sat back in his seat, stunned as everything—the long hours at the clinic, weight loss and lack of sleep— dropped on him all at once. Trey narrowed his eyes and sat up. He wanted his life, his woman and his peace back. "Damn," he said out loud. "J, you're right."

Jared waved a hand at the beer vendor stationed a few feet away.

"Two Coronas," his friend ordered.

Once the ice-cold bottle was in his hand, Trey tapped the bottle against Jared's. "I'm getting her back, man."

"Thank god. Now can I enjoy the last few minutes of the game? And you might as well give me the hundred dollars now."

Trey's brow furrowed with confusion. "We only bet for fifty."

"Jo's going to give you fifty tomorrow."

"He bet on the game, too?"

"Nah, he said he'd pay me fifty dollars if I could get you to make up with Sasha. Seems that you've been a cranky SOB at the clinic since she broke up with you."

Trey laughed until his eyes watered, and then pulled out his wallet and handed over the Benjamin.

When the doorbell rang, Sasha dropped her pen on the desk at Darwin's first bark. "I'll get it!" she yelled out, forgetting that Jackson was off skiing in Vail. She'd spent the past week hiding in the house and spending time going over grant requests, financial documents and research documents. She'd done everything that she could do not to think about Trey. But that didn't keep him from slipping into her dreams at night and leaving her feeling depressed and lonely when she woke in the morning.

She walked through the house and looked through the peephole and saw nothing. She pulled open the door, looked down, and her mouth dropped as a little four-legged body trotted between her legs. Little Ralph had grown at least two inches since she'd last seen him at Trey's parents' house.

Sasha stepped outside and scanned the area looking for Trey. Her eyes narrowed and she mumbled, "Coward."

Shutting the door, she turned to see Darwin and the puppy roughhousing in the middle of the floor. It took her a moment to see the note tied to his collar. She walked over and leaned down. Being careful not to startle Ralph, she held his wiggling squirming body for a second and released the small note. She unrolled it slowly and her heart caught at the childlike writing.

Homeless. Can I come in? If yes, open the door.

She ran to the door, put her hand on the knob and hesitated slightly before pulling back. His coming to her didn't mean that he was ready to make the commitment she wanted. What if she was only setting herself up for more heartache? Sasha put her head against the door and closed her eyes. She'd spent the latter half of her adult life never feeling as though being alone meant that she was less complete. Years ago, she had her first taste of love and the sweetness of it had been so good until the bitter aftertaste of being alone again had knocked her to her knees. And here she was again on the verge of having her heart broken again.

"Come on, sweetheart. Open the door."

"I can't," she replied.

"It's cold out here."

"Then go away."

"Where would I go?"

"I don't care. Just leave me alone."

"You don't mean that."

She bit her tongue to quell the instinctive reply, because he was right. She didn't mean it and she never would. Regardless of how everything turned out and the massive amounts of ice cream she consumed and tears she'd shed since her parents had left, there would always be a part of her that would care about Trey Blackfox.

"Sasha, I put the loft on the market yesterday and it sold this morning."

She blinked twice and then pulled back the door. The frigid air curled her sock-covered toes. "What?"

Trey stepped through the doorway, and his heart pounded as Sasha turned around. The cloud of pain in her eyes made him want to drop to his knees. He drank in the sight of her standing there in a robe and fuzzy white socks. Ralph trotted over and Trey automatically bent down to pick up the puppy and settled him against his chest. "The real estate agent dropped by with the papers an hour ago."

"I guess the real estate market is hotter than you thought."

"No, my uncle decided to move to Atlanta and he thought that the loft would be a great place to start over."

"Midlife crisis?"

Trey shook his head and smiled. "Uncle James has never married and he's coming down here to find a wife who would be willing to put up with cigar smoking, and willing to give him four kids."

Several heartbeats passed before she spoke. "So where are you moving?"

"I don't know yet. But this time I want to build a house."

His hand stilled as he rubbed Ralph's head. "I love you, Sasha. I don't *think* it. I *know* it. I've never loved a woman so much. Everything else in my life has gone to hell since you've been gone. I love your strength. I love you. I want to wake up with you sprawled across half the bed, see you grow big with our child, hear you scream at me when you have hot flashes and cry on my shoulders at weddings. Once a Blackfox makes a commitment, we keep it for life. You are my life, baby. Say you'll be my wife."

He said all the right words and her heart filled to the point where she imagined that it might burst. It wasn't just the words. It was the way he looked at her. The look in his eyes was more powerful and compelling than any words he could have spoken. Because what was in those brown eyes that she loved was pure and honest. He looked at her as if she were his sustenance, and that he'd die without the taste of it.

Sasha took a step forward and cupped his face with her hands. "I love you," she said in a soft, hoarse voice.

Trey smiled. "I love you, Darwin, Zaza, Ralph, Jackson, your mother, your father and your toes."

She kissed him to still his mouth. "Jackson's off skiing and we've got the house to ourselves. How about you leave Ralph with Darwin and show me how much you missed me?" she asked in a sultry voice.

"You sure? He's not exactly housebroken."

"Trey. Take me to bed."

He needed no more instruction than that. He took Sasha in his arms and carried her up the stairs. With each step he thanked God for his family and friends, but most of all he was thankful for the lady in his arms.

Big-boned beauty, Chere Adams
plunges headfirst into an
extreme makeover to impress
fitness fanatic
Quentin Abrahams.

But perhaps it's Chere's curves that
have caught Quentin's eye?

All About Me

Marcia King-Gamble

REQUEST YOUR FREE BOOKS!

2 FREE NOVELS
PLUS 2 FREE GIFTS!

KIMANI™
ROMANCE

Love's ultimate destination!